One Dead Preacher

A David Price Mystery

One Dead Preacher

A David Price Mystery

by

TONY LINDSAY

Q-Boro Books

An Urban Entertainment Company

Published by Q-Boro Books

ISBN-13: 978-0-7394-8062-5

Printed in the United States of America

Cover Layout & Design—Candace K. Cottrell
Editors—Melissa Forbes, Stacey Seay, Candace K. Cottrell

Q-BORO BOOKS
Jamaica, Queens NY 11434

Dedicated to Professor and Poet, Sterling Plump, who saw the writer in me. Love to you and yours.

One Dead Preacher

A David Price Mystery

One

I often want to be the man my ex-wife and my mother want me to be: a solid guy, a good, Christian brother who comes straight home on payday, who doesn't know where the floating crap game is, who doesn't know who's got the good weed or which chick gives the best head—just a regular Joe, like my old man.

My dad had no use for the streets or the people in them. Solid as a rock. I'd bet my right arm that he never cheated on my mother. The man got up at 3:45 AM Monday through Friday for thirty years. Thirty years. I'd pass him in the mornings, me coming in, him going out.

He'd ask me, "Ain't you tired of them streets yet, boy?"

I would tell him no. But if he were to ask me that question now, some twenty years later, my answer would be yes, without a doubt.

In the past, the streets had always been my refuge, my place to go when I needed life to make sense. I knew what to expect from street life. It was the "normal life" that kept me banging my head against the wall.

If I was more like my old man, I wouldn't be lying here breathing oxygen through a mask with .22 caliber bullet holes in my chest, my neck, and I hope to God in my thigh, and not in my jones. My neck is bandaged so I can't look down, but she was aiming at my jones. I think I put my thigh in the way, but I ain't really sure. I ain't prayed in four years, but when I woke up in this hospital room, I asked God to let it be my thigh and not my jones. Everything hurts, so I can't really tell. When I piss I don't know where it's going or where it's coming from. The nurse put the television on the Christian station. I guess she heard me calling Jesus and figured I was a Christian.

I called him. I didn't know who else to call. It's funny how you fall back to what you were raised on when your ass is out. She wanted to kill me; probably thought she did. As soon as the cops come, I'm turning her in. I've never told the police on anyone in my life, but she tried to shoot my jones off, and maybe she did. God, I hope it's there.

The last time I was in the hospital I had self-administering painkillers. I heard the doctor tell the nurse no painkillers this time because of my heart. I hope she didn't shoot me in the heart. I'm not that wealthy, and hearts cost money. That would be some shit if she shot me in the heart and my jones. I'm sorta glad I feel the pain, because I once heard paralyzed people don't feel pain. I can't move nothing, but everything hurts. The last thing I remember was her standing over me, aiming at my jones.

It was about five AM, three days ago, and I was on a good roll—five naturals in a row. I passed the dice most of the night, but suddenly I felt lucky. It's a hard feeling to describe. I get very confident and full of myself. I feel a little taller, a little better looking, a bit more aggressive. It's a lot like catching the eye of an attractive woman, whose glance returns your interest—the sudden confidence that surges through you and puts everything in sync. The rhythm of my walk, the tone of my speech, the depth of my sight—they're all affected, all improved.

I blew into the small opening between the thumb and forefinger of my left fist. I rolled the dice with my left hand. I heard the craps clacking in my ear. I blew again and shook them some more. I tightened my fist and the clacking progressed to clicking, I was about to roll my sixth natural when I felt it. I got a tap on the shoulder. I ignored it. Whoever it was would feel my wrath later. Again, a tap. I waved back with my right hand to push the person off me and I stopped. When I pushed back with my right hand I gripped a thigh, a firm thigh covered in silk, not nylon. My ex-wife wore silk. This was a firm, thin, but meaty thigh. It wasn't bone my hand was gripping. I remained down on my left knee and re-shook the dice. I didn't release the thigh or turn around. I rolled out my sixth straight seven. After one box car and a snake eye blessed me, I turned around to see the face that was attached to the thigh I held.

I am far from gullible when it comes to beauty. Seldom am I awestruck or left speechless at seeing a woman's face, but the face I looked up into that morning kept me on my knee. I truly wanted to stand, but I couldn't. I could do nothing but stare at her.

There must have been about twenty men in the garage that morning. This garage was one of Ricky's better locations. Anchored to the center of the floor was a circular slate covered with red felt. The men stood and kneeled around the slate. Everything smokeable was smoked in the garage. Language was not restricted. I was called everything but a child of God due to the six naturals I threw, but I heard little of it. I only heard my own heartbeat. All I saw was her face. All I smelled were lilacs. All

I felt was the silk. She didn't move her thigh, and she didn't take her eyes from mine.

"I need to talk to you, Mr. Price. Ricky said you could help me." Her voice was barely above a whisper, but I heard it.

I released her thigh and stood.

"One second, baby." I was trying to regain my cool. I turned back to the circle and collected my winnings. The six naturals got me a little over eighteen hundred. I peeled off a hundred and eighty for the house man, Ricky. When I handed him the cash, I bent down to his ear. "What's up with the babe?"

Ricky was still working, watching the dice and cutting on sixes and eights. He turned to me quickly.

"She's in a spot. I ain't got time for all the details. Help her out. Bill me if you got to. Come by my house in the afternoon, and I'll give you the scoop. Keep her safe until then."

He went back to the game. I stood. Ricky had more than enough thugs in his employ to watch a girl. There was more to it, and I knew it. I looked down at the back of his finger-waved hair and knew he was pulling me into some mess. Over the thirty years I'd known Ricky, he had never volunteered to pay for anything. The woman was a good ten steps away. I smelled the lilacs. I went to her, put my hand on the small of her back, and said, "Come with me."

When I go out to nightclubs, I wear a pinky diamond ring, a gold Rolex, a gold link neck chain, and a couple of nugget bracelets. It impresses some women. Outside of wedding bands, I rarely notice a woman's jewelry, but this woman was laced. Her right wrist alone held four or five diamond tennis bracelets. Each pinky and ring finger had two-carat clusters. The gold chain around her neck held a simple, I'm guessing, three-carat marquis diamond.

My taste in women over the years has changed. As a young man, about nineteen or twenty, I liked them slim, dark, and petite; in my early twenties—slim, tall, and dark; mid twenties—healthy and dark, until I met my ex-wife, who is as yellow as a banana and as thin as a rail. As of late, I have no physical preference. I like them neat, clean, well-dressed, well-read, and socially conscious. I look for women I can talk about things with: social issues, race issues, sports, literary works, environmental issues, black art, plays, music, any and everything. I had been looking for a woman with a mind. I thought I was getting away from the physical, until I laid my eyes on her. If she was brain dead and couldn't speak a word, I would have helped her, and for one reason only. She was fine.

Maybe it's sexist, I don't know, but I like women in dresses and skirts. I like them better when the dresses and skirts are long with splits, preferably with hidden splits, the kinds that fold over in the middle. There's something about a long skirt with a split. When a woman takes a step and for a brief second you see that thigh, damn! That gets my attention. This woman was wearing a long, black dress down to her ankles with a split in the middle.

I drive a Fleetwood Brougham. It's my third Cadillac. I know what people say about blacks and Cadillacs, and for me it's partially true. There was a time when I lived in my Cadillac, and I have paid my car note before I paid my mortgage. I'm aware that it's not wise to love things, but I loved all my Cadillacs, and I am especially fond of this one.

All my life I've heard people talk about foolish black men and their Cadillacs. I have come to one conclusion: they have never owned one. They have never seen a father's face light up with pride when his son pulls into the church lot for Sunday morning service, driving a new Cadillac. They have never seen the envy on a man's face when they pass his lesser car on the highway or park next to him at a Bulls' game. They have never felt the gentle but powerful push of its V8 engine on the highway heading to Atlanta. They most certainly haven't seen the sparkle in a woman's eyes when the front door of the luxurious sedan is opened for her. Yes, I drive a Cadillac, and that morning, minus my jewelry because I never wear it to crap games, I was oh so proud of my '96, pearl white, Fleetwood Brougham.

I held the door open for her and noticed that I stood head and shoulders above her. I'd mistaken her scent. Not lilacs, but the smell of roses filled my head. Her black hair was cropped close—thick, natural looking curls in a short, round afro. It couldn't have been an inch long. I wanted to rub my chin in those curls. She didn't reach for the door handle when she slipped in the car. She extended her hand to me. I was to be her brace. Once in, she crossed her legs at the ankles, looked up at me with ebony black eyes, and said, "Thank you, Mr. Price," in a tissue paper light voice.

"No problem, baby." I closed the Fleetwood Brougham door with a slight push of an open hand. I walked in front of the car for two reasons. One, I wanted her to get a good look at me. I'm not a bad looking brother. I dress well and I stay in good shape. Two, I needed a couple of seconds to think. I needed to know what Ricky was getting me into, but I didn't want to bombard her with questions. I also didn't want her mind on a bad situation. I wanted her slender face smiling. Ricky said she was in a spot. Whatever the situation, barring the death of a loved one, it could wait until the afternoon. I wanted to hear about her. I wanted to know where she was born, if she was married, did she have any kids, and did she like men. My plan was simple. I wouldn't ask her why she needed help.

While starting the Brougham, I told her I was going to Jackie's for breakfast and I asked if she was hungry. I figured that if she said yes, the situation wasn't that bad. Most people can't eat when they are seriously troubled.

"Jackie's on Seventy-first Street?" She was familiar with the south side. That was a good sign. Maybe she was from Chicago. I enjoyed Chicago women. We always had something to talk about.

"You know the place?" I pulled out of my parking space and headed north down Ninety-second and Ada.

"Mmph, mmph. I been there before." She spoke with a rhythm. At least I heard rhythm.

"You feel like going now?" Jackie's was one of the few soul food restaurants that were open twenty-four hours. I ate at the place more than I ate at home. They had some real good food—potatoes in the string beans, fat back in the greens, big slices of sweet potato pie, short ribs, fried catfish—it was all good.

"No, not really." She opened her window halfway and let in the early morning air. Even though it was mid July, the city hadn't heated up yet. The air was great in the early morning. People who said there was no fresh air in the city were not out at the right time. It was unintentional, but I sighed when she said she didn't want to go to Jackie's.

"I would rather go to the IHOP on Western," she said in response to my sigh.

"Not a problem. You like pancakes?"

"I love them. I really like IHOP's blueberry ones." I saw a small smile growing.

She liked to eat. She knew about Jackie's and IHOP, both of which are late night places to eat. Baby girl had hung out a little bit.

"You go there often?"

"My husband and I used to, but not anymore." The smile on her face died. I guessed her husband was the problem.

"Well, last month they added a couple of other berries to the menu," I lied, but I wanted that growing smile back.

"Really?"

"Yeah. Blackberry, cherry, raspberry, a whole bunch of them."

"Cherries are not berries."

"Well you know what I mean." The smile was back. "You want to hear some music?"

"No. I want to hear about you. Ricky thinks the world of you." She turned to face me with that sentence.

Ricky and I were thirty-year friends. There was no telling what he told baby girl about me. It all depended on what he wanted from her. I should have pushed him for more information.

She didn't want to talk about her situation either. That was more than cool with me. I tried not to stare at the cleavage her healthy breasts formed, but my eyes wouldn't listen.

"I'm sorry, baby, what did you say?" She saw me looking at her cleavage, so I didn't hide my distraction.

"I said, tell me about you." Her full lips were smiling, but her eyes were inquiring. There was little traffic on Ninety-fifth Street. I cruised up to the stoplight on Damen Avenue. I deliberately drove slowly to spot any tails. I didn't know how much trouble she was in or with whom. I had to watch my back. Women who wore as much jewelry as she did were seldom in a *little* trouble. I guessed that her husband was causing her problems, and if he adorned her so, he didn't want to see her leave. Jewelry store robberies were in the news and those robbers were also killers. At last count, four owners and two clerks were dead.

"Ain't much to tell. Besides, ladies first."

"What do you want to know?" she asked. What I really wanted to know was what she was to Ricky. I knew most of his serious babes on the side. If he cared about this honey, he should have told me more. It wouldn't be my fault if she and I got together.

"Everything, starting with your kindergarten teacher. Was she fat? Did she spank y'all with a ruler?" She laughed a good, deep down laugh, the kind that relieves. I was proud of myself for giving it to her. She placed her dainty hand on my shoulder. That was another good sign. She was a person who liked to touch.

"Kindergarten is a bit far back. Let's start with high school."

"That's fine with me, but I don't want to hear about your boyfriends." I spotted a green sedan in the rearview mirror. It wasn't gaining, which meant it was traveling as slow as we were.

"Very few in high school, but I can't tell you about high school without talking about them."

"OK, but no descriptions. I'm insecure," I said, grinning and showing all of my thirty-two pearly whites.

"I doubt that."

"Why?"

"Because of the way you carry yourself. You know you look good." Another good sign, flattery. Women not afraid to compliment a brother definitely scored high in my book. Baby girl was in play.

"Thank you, but you look better."

"I'm supposed to," she said with pride.

"Well now, tell me what you want me to know, girl!" The smile was full grown and warm. The green sedan passed us at Western Avenue. It contained two young boys trying to light a blunt, marijuana rolled in a cigar leaf. Their loud music broke through the quiet murmur of the city's early morning. The heavy bass line seemed to be trying to kick free of their trunk.

"When I was a freshman," she began, "I played volleyball on the varsity team. I was good. The first game, I got my period on the court in front of fifty people. I was embarrassed, so I quit. That's it for freshman year. In my sophomore year, I had a crush on the football coach. He broke my heart when he told me to come back when I was twenty-five. In my junior year, I lost my virginity to the captain of the football team after a homecoming defeat. I felt sorry for him. In my senior year, I got pregnant and miscarried. I graduated with my class and went to the Art Institute. That's enough for now. Your turn."

She was so intimate, so fast that she caught me off guard. Heartbreak, pain, and embarrassment were all remembered with a slight smile. I kissed her hand, which was still on my shoulder, as I pulled into IHOP's parking lot.

"After we eat, I'll tell you my story."

She was determined not to wait until after breakfast to hear my story. She started questioning me as soon as we were seated.

"Do you remember your kindergarten teacher?"

"Well, you know it wasn't last year. I got to reach back a little further than you."

"Not much further."

She was smiling again. Aged copper was the color of

her skin, like an old penny. If she was close to my age, it didn't show. Usually when people get as close to forty as I was, they were missing a couple of teeth, showing a little gray, growing a little gut, developing that second chin, and the bright white gleam of youth has left their eyes. Her eyes held a gleam. She had only one slender chin and a long, thin neck. If she was missing any teeth, it didn't show in her smile, and I saw not the slightest beginning of a gut. I guessed she was in her late twenties or early thirties. I ordered blueberry pancakes for her and a Denver omelet for myself. While eating, I wanted to call her by her name, but realized I didn't know it.

"What's your whole name, baby?" I asked, saving myself the embarrassment of not knowing her name.

"Well, I was Sugar Greer up until a year ago. Now I'm Sugar Owens, but soon to return to Sugar Greer." I watched her mind drift from the table to a place that took the pleasantness from her face.

"Your mother named you Sugar?" I asked, trying to bring her back.

"No, my father. My mother wanted to name me Melody."

"I like Sugar."

"Me, the name, or sugar?"

"All of them."

Her face remained serious.

"How much did Ricky tell you about my situation?"

"Not much." She was ready to talk, but I wasn't. "Where do you know Ricky from?"

"He's married to my sister." After she finished the pancakes, she pushed away the coffee cup the waitress had filled. I should have recognized the name Greer, but I saw no family resemblance between Sugar and Ricky's wife, Martha.

"You're Martha's sister?" She nodded.

"You know Martha?"

"Yeah, I know her. I been knowing her for years, before her and Ricky got married. I was the best man at their wedding. Their oldest son is named after me." I decided not to ask why she wasn't at the wedding. I remembered Ricky being upset at one of the bridesmaids for disappointing Martha.

"No, David was my daddy's name. Martha named him after our father, David Jerome."

"Are you sure about that?"

"I know my daddy's name."

"I'm sure you do, but are you sure they named the boy after him?"

"Is your middle name Jerome?"

"No."

"Well that answers that," she said in a curt tone. I ignored the tone.

"Lying ass Ricky. He told me he named the boy after me." I had to chuckle. Little David was twenty years old and out of Ricky's six kids, he was my favorite. I bought the boy's school clothes all through school, paid a good part of his first year's college tuition, and gave him one of my Cadillacs when he graduated from high school. For twenty years, I believed that boy was my namesake. I couldn't wait to set Ricky straight about it. "Named after your daddy, humph, ain't that something?"

"Mr. Price?"

"David. Mr. Price is my father."

"David, I'm not sure you can help me. I need protection."

"That's my business, Sugar. I protect people." I sipped my cold coffee. The waitress hadn't freshened mine. I guess she figured baby girl was paying the tab.

"You're a bodyguard?"

"Sort of. I'm not licensed as a bodyguard. The state

wouldn't license me as one so I run a security escort service. They had no problem with me being a security guard."

"Are you good at being a bodyguard?"

"The best in the business." I beckoned the chubby sister over for some fresh brew. She ignored me.

"Were you in the Secret Service or the CIA?"

"No." I laughed a bit. People watched too many movies. Most bodyguards were not former Secret Service or CIA agents.

"Where were you trained?"

"The streets of Chicago." She cast her eyes down, doubting my ability. "Baby, if you need protection in this city, I'm your man. I know Chicago like the back of my hand. I was born and raised in it and I ain't never left it. I know people from Glencoe to Gary. No one can keep you safer."

"But you don't carry a gun," she said, looking back at me.

"Why do you say that?" I couldn't stop the grin.

"I looked."

"Those big, pretty eyes are untrained. I carry three guns." I caught the waitress's eye and held my cup up, pleading. She smiled and nodded.

"Where?"

"Where they belong. Hidden." I placed my hand on top of Sugar's.

She slid her hand back.

"How much do you charge?"

"How long do you need me?" The waitress filled my cup, and the coffee was fresh and strong. I thanked her with a wink and a smile.

"Maybe two weeks."

Her words warmed me better than a shot of Old Grand-Dad. In two weeks, I would know all about her. She wouldn't be out of my sight.

"Well, two weeks is a long assignment. Maybe I should assign you to one of my other escorts?" I blew into my cup, avoiding her eyes, but listening to her tone.

"Ricky said *you* would help me."

"I know, but I'm the president of the company. I've got a lot of responsibilities." I was lying. I did have a heavy caseload, but the five security escorts I had working under me were handling it fine. Most of my days at the office were spent twiddling my thumbs. Carol, who was my first real client, now ran the office. She answered the phone, ordered supplies, assigned cases, and brought in more new clients than I did. I needed something to do and I wanted to be around Sugar.

"You don't want to work with me?" Those ebony stones encased in pure ivory didn't blink when she asked. There was no denying she had beautiful eyes, but it was more than the look of them that held me. It was the depth of them. They seemed to go deep inside of her past lies, past facades.

"No, it's not that. It's just that if you doubt my ability, you won't listen and you won't do what I tell you to do. You have to feel safe with me for me to protect you, and it sounds like you might not feel safe with me. You might feel safer with someone else." I sipped my brew. I didn't want her to beg, but I wanted her to remember that she came looking for my help. There was no doubt in my mind that I was taking her case. There was no way she was getting away from me, but I had no intention of starting out by kissing her ass.

"I haven't felt safe in weeks. I haven't laughed in months. I haven't eaten in days. I laughed this morning and I ate. I would be lying if I said I didn't feel safe with you, Mr. Price, David. It's just that you seem like such a nice guy and I didn't see your gun. The people I'm afraid of are not nice guys and I've seen their guns." Her thin eyebrows scrunched up as she spoke and sat back in the booth. "I would hate for you to be hurt because of me. I have hurt enough people in this lifetime."

I started grinning. She thought I was too nice and she didn't believe I had guns.

"This isn't funny," she said.

I watched her slender face become stern. She shook her head from side-to-side in small, tight movements. She assumed I wasn't taking her seriously. I forced the grin from my face.

"I didn't say it was funny, Sugar, but it's been awhile since someone thought I was too nice, especially a woman. I'm gonna take your case and I hope when we're done you still think I'm nice." I looked down at my watch. It was seven AM. "It's too early to go over to Ricky's, and I'm tired. No one appears to be following you now, so the safest place for you is a place you've never been before. I need to rest and I feel safest at my place." I stopped without asking the question. I didn't ask her because I didn't want to hear her say no. Although romance was on my mind, I did need to rest, and she needed to be safe.

"You didn't say how much your protection would cost."

"Ricky told me to bill him. Believe me, Sugar, after the information about David, he will be well billed."

"When you say 'your place,' are you speaking of your home or some safe house you keep for situations such as this?" She picked up the bill, read it, and kept her eyes down while she asked the question.

"My home is my safe house," I said, standing. Being six feet, two inches, standing is better when you're selling protection. I pulled out the knot I won at the crap game and peeled off a twenty and a ten. The bill was less than twenty. I wanted her to see me tipping. A big tipper impresses some women.

"Really?"

"Really."

"How safe?"

"It's state of the art in home security. A fly couldn't enter without me knowing."

"And once it enters, do you have a swatter?"

"Yeah, I got something for it."

"Is it big?"

"What?"

"Your swatter?"

"Huh?" Again she caught me off guard. She switched directions in midstream like an eel. Normally I'm adept at word games, but I wasn't expecting it from her. Now it was her turn to grin as she stood.

I have a love/hate relationship with mixed signals from women. I loved the allure, the possibility that she was signaling consent. I hated the tease, the woman who gave signals merely for the sake of prompting a response, switched her butt just for the pleasure of having me follow her down the street. Word games were mixed signals. Swatter could have meant a fly swatter, or she could have been asking about my jones. Playing the game gave her the option of playing innocent. If she decided romance with me was not on her agenda, she could say she was talking about a fly swatter, and act offended by me assuming she was talking about my jones. I've learned the safest response to a word game is a smile, and then I wait for the next signal. Misreading a mixed signal has often left me with egg on my face.

I lived in the inner city, or more precisely, in the hood, in the house my grandmama left to my brothers and me. My oldest brother, the rich Republican, didn't want the responsibility of renting a house in the hood. The brother closest to me in age also wanted to sell the house. He was always in need of cash. After my divorce was final, not only in court but in my mind as well, I moved out of the studio apartment I rented in Harvey and bought my brothers' shares in the house. I loved the house and the neighborhood it was in. My house was located on Sixty-first and Throop Street. The neighborhood was not what it used to be, but neither was I. It could be a dangerous place, but it was where I felt comfortable. It was where I chose to live.

Sugar faced me for most of the drive. She avoided talking about the specifics of her situation. All she was willing to tell me was that her husband was the threat. They were married for more than a year, but he'd changed over the past few months. He became jealous, possessive, and threatening. He slapped her yesterday, and she'd been running ever since. I didn't ask if his actions were justified—no woman deserves to be beaten—but a woman as beautiful as Sugar could easily make a man jealous or make him lose control. Insecurity often takes form in jealousy, and a man would have to be a god not to feel insecure around her. If she was physically flawed, it was hidden as well as my guns.

"Here we are. This is my humble abode."

I'm far from humble about the house. I spent a lot of money getting it remodeled—ceilings raised and removed, walls knocked down, rooms expanded and added. The basement was converted into an underground garage allowing me to pull directly in from the street. There was no garage door opener. A recognition chip was installed in the dash of all my Cadillacs. When I drove up, the garage door opened. It impressed some women.

Once you were in the garage, you were in. The door shut and locked, and you were in total darkness. The lights were activated by voice command.

"Lights please, Wilma." The garage instantly flooded with enough light to perform surgery.

"That's smooth, Mr. Man," she said, blinking her eyes. "Why so much light?"

"Security mainly, but I do a little work on my cars and I like my work area well lit. It also has a sobering effect when I come home a little buzzed."

"I'm sure it does."

I opened her door and helped her out. I liked to show off my house. The technology and the interior design always surprised people.

"OK, Sugar, pretend you were trying to break into my humble abode. Use anything you like."

"Anything?"

"Yes. Please feel free."

"Hand me your keys."

"My keys?"

"Yeah. You said anything." Again she was smiling, this time like a child who thought she'd outsmarted her parent.

"OK, fine." She took the keys and walked over to the only door. She slipped her Gucci shoulder bag around her neck.

"There is no lock or keyhole."

"Really."

"OK, smart guy, I'm not done yet." She stomped on the rubber mat in front of the door, and pushed against the metal door with serious force. She stepped back. "There are no hinges, no key card slot, nothing. What is it, a phony door?"

"No, that's the door, baby." She smiled.

"I got it! Open the door, Wilma. Damn. OK, I give." She was almost pouting. I knew the pout was for me. It was one of those sexy, sly pouts, a brat's pout on a woman too old to be a brat, but I liked it.

"You sure? You got my keys. You should be able to get into my house."

"I can't get into your house, David. It is a very secure house. You obviously know your business. I should not have doubted you earlier. Happy?"

"Yeah."

"Good, because I have to use the bathroom."

She had the right idea, but she just didn't look in the right place. The entry slot was on the right side of the door jam.

"Like I said, you had my keys." It was my turn to grin.

After she used the bathroom, I gave her the grand tour. If she was impressed, she didn't show it, and that kinda pissed me off. When I said I spent a lot of money remodeling my grandmama's house, I meant a lot of money. I had the dining room wall knocked down to form one large living area. My high beams were exposed, track lights hung along the walls, and my prints were encased in glass at a waist-high view. The living area held two brown, leather recliners, a leather sofa that could seat six, and a digital surround sound entertainment center with a fifty-two inch screen. My place was laid. I designed it to impress, and she didn't even blink. I wasn't going to ask if she liked it. I never had to ask anyone in the past. What she said next almost made me throw her out.

"God, David, what designer ripped you off? Don't tell me. I know it was Tammy Lynn. I recognize her style. She turns everything into a loft. Beautifully built frame houses like this were meant to have rooms, especially dining rooms. That's part of their charm. Tammy doesn't appreciate historical design. If she had her way, we would all live in factories."

"What?" I replied.

"Was Tammy Lynn your designer?"

"Yeah."

"And I know she charged you a fortune to gut it like this."

"Gut it?"

"Yes. That's all she did. She gutted it! She tore down the walls and removed the ceilings. This was a house, David. It was built to be a home, not a shoe factory. Why didn't Martha refer you to me?"

"I didn't tell her I was working on the house." When we walked into the room I had put the lights on dim. I was going to create a mood, but now I switched them to bright. Obviously she wasn't seeing the place right. Minnie Ripperton's *Perfect Angel* CD was in my hand, but I also changed my mind about that.

"You take her to court?"

"No!"

"You should. She's a criminal, a con artist, a disgrace to residential interior designers. And another thing, David, why would you spend so much money on a house located in the slums? Englewood has been dead for years. There's no regentrification happening anywhere close to here. White people and black people with money are afraid of Englewood. God, I hope you don't run your business like you invest in real estate. Do you have anything to drink?" Her siddity tone clicked in my head and tightened my jaws. She sounded like my ex-mother in-law.

I liked my house. No, I loved my house, and I wasn't too pleased about her calling it a shoe factory.

"It ain't that bad, Sugar." I sat on the couch, ignoring her request for a drink. Fine or not, I wasn't about to serve her my booze and get my home insulted. A line had to be drawn. "The designer was following my instructions."

"No, that's not the way it goes. You pay a designer for their expertise." She sat on the couch next to me and looked at me so earnestly I had to listen.

"Any designer worth their weight in salt respects architectural design and they pass that respect on to their client. Let me guess. You like space?"

"Yes, I like my space, I like room to breathe."

"I understand that. That could have been accomplished without gutting your home. You lost your attic, your dining room, your sun porch and I'm guessing your foyer. For what, one big room? You can sit here and tell me it was your idea, but remember, I asked you about Tammy Lynn. Don't get me wrong, it's charming in a lofty way, but it could have been so much more. You needed a sister's touch. Men don't design with families in mind. It's not your fault." She placed her hand on my knee. I moved my knee away.

"What do you mean?"

"For example, take Christmas dinner. You have no formal dining area. The house was designed with one, but that function is gone. Yes, this is a cool spot for a bachelor but even a suave guy like you gets caught. Once that happens, believe me, a dining room is sure to follow." She rested her head on my shoulder. "What about that drink? I know you have cognac."

She was doing it again, switching directions in midstream. How could a person insult a man's home, and then ask him for a drink; tell him his home looked like a shoe factory, and then rest her head on his shoulder? A truly suave guy would have gotten up, fixed her a drink, and served it with a smile. I slid away from her.

How could she talk about my place like that? This was my grandmama's house. Sure, I made changes, but changes for the better, improvements. It took me two months to strip, stain, and shellac the floors. I went to every carpet retailer, wholesaler, and showroom in the state to find a carpet and rug to match my brushed lambskin couches and recliners. I spent weeks at Merchandise Mart searching for my coffee and end tables. A Jamaican brother I flew in from Texas handcrafted my bookcases. The track lights were ordered specially from Germany. Yes, Ms. Tammy Lynn cost me a small fortune, but it was all worth it. It was for my place, my space, my home. If I got up and fixed her a drink, it would'a been a small miracle. I told her little residential interior designer self how to open the hidden bar at the bottom of my bookcase, and sat back on my couch.

She didn't make a move toward the bookcase. Instead, she slid off her black, spike-heeled shoes, stretched out on the couch, and placed her head in my lap. She looked up at me with a pair of eyes and a smile that promised paradise.

"Oh, David, please. I'm so tired, and I don't want to ramble through your bar looking for ice and glasses." She adjusted her small head against my thigh. "Be a dear. Remy Martin with one cube of ice, OK?" I smelled the lilacs. I saw the unblemished skin at the top of her breasts. I felt the lightness of her head resting on my thigh. I watched those copper-colored eyelids with thin lashes, cover the brightest, softest eyes I'd seen in my adult life, but I didn't move.

"Ain't that much to ramble through. And what makes you think there would be ice or Remy in a shoe factory? I might have a little E&J and a couple paper cups." I wasn't getting her a gotdamn thing, pretty eyes or not.

"Now, Mr. David Price, I know you not only have Remy, but Remy Martin V.S.O.P. And I'm sure you'll be serving it in a lead crystal snifter. I was not insulting *your* style, or *your* sophistication. My insult, if you felt one, was aimed at your designer, not you. Please forgive my candor. You have a beautiful home, but I would have done this area differently. I love the rest of your home. I was intrigued by your choice of eighteenth century furnishings in the master bedroom. That was a robust, adventurous, and industrialist period in our country's history. I was more than intrigued. To be honest, Mr. Man, I was impressed. You have a great deal of taste." She wasn't smiling, but the allure was in her voice. "Now, sir," she said, sitting up, "that is as close as I get to an apology. Happy?"

"Yeah."

Watching her sip the drink I fixed, I was again taken by her beauty. I literally stared at her. I could not have dreamed up a more beautiful woman. I stood up before I made a fool of myself. I was on the verge of asking stupid questions, questions a grown man of thirty-eight shouldn't ask. Can I kiss you? Do you think I'm attractive? How old are you? Can I see your titties? Will you sleep with me if I keep my drawers on?

I found myself standing with no real purpose. Out of habit, I walked to the wall and dimmed the lights. I walked back to the couch and put my hand on her shoulder.

"Sugar, I got a couple calls to make. My eighteenth-century bedroom is all yours. You know where it is. I'm calling it a night."

"But you didn't finish your drink, and we hardly talked. Are you still upset?" She placed her hand on top of mine and pulled me around to the front of the couch to face her. My mother told me a woman's glory is in the beauty of her hair, but she'd never looked into Sugar Greer's eyes.

"Naw, baby," I said, sitting on the couch. "Not at all. Everyone is entitled to an opinion. Your apology was accepted, but I know you're tired." Maybe it was the brightness of the whites, the richness of the black, or the teardrop shape, but her eyes were holding me again.

"I'm not tired, and you still haven't told me about yourself."

It wasn't that she wanted to hear about me. I heard fear in her voice. She didn't want to be alone. People, myself included, are funny. We avoid bad situations until they are unavoidable. If I left her alone, she would have no choice but to think about her situation. I got up to fix myself a drink.

"What do you want to know?" I poured myself straight shots while she watched me fix the drinks. Men who drink straight shots impress some women.

"I know most of it."

"Really?"

"Yep, you're easy to read."

"Tell me what you think you know." I sipped my drink and sat back.

"You won't get insulted?"

"No," I said with certainty, but I was far from certain.

"I'm only guessing."

"Go on."

"You're not married, probably divorced. You have children. My guess is teenagers or young adults. I saw the baseball stuff in the corner. You weren't in the military. You said you never lived outside the city. You like being around your people. There is no other reason for living in Englewood. You're materialistic—the Caddy, the furniture, your clothes. I'm certain you're a Virgo, because sex is all in your eyes. Ain't no man as horny as a Virgo man. How am I doing so far?" I sat up.

"Materialistic?"

"Don't deny it, David." She held up her hand like a crossing guard. "There is nothing wrong with having nice things. More of our people should be materialistic."

"Having nice things does not make me materialistic." I sipped the Remy and tapped the crystal lead snifter with my index finger.

"No, but using them to impress does."

"You got to explain that." I placed the snifter on an ostrich skin coaster and picked up the surround sound remote from the coffee table. Erykah Badu was in disc one. I pushed play and smiled at Sugar when Erykah's voice joined us.

"You're a showoff. You showed me all your stuff before you told me one real thing about yourself. You put your possessions and your business accomplishments out front. You want people to see your stuff before they see you. If it weren't for the things Ricky told me about you, I wouldn't trust you. You are materialistic."

"What did Ricky tell you about me?" It wasn't the first time a sister had called me materialistic. I always took it as a compliment. I picked up the snifter, sat back, and enjoyed the cool feeling that came with Erykah Badu. My drink was stiffer than I wanted it. I regretted not dropping a cube of ice in my Remy, but a mood was developing and I didn't want to endanger it by standing.

"Oh no, you're supposed to tell me about you. After all, you're my protector, my security escort." She leaned against the far arm of my couch and swung her feet into my lap. "Start talking." Her head swayed to Erykah's "On and On."

"Horny, huh?" I knew where asking that would lead, but I was on automatic—the Remy, the dim lights, her pretty little feet in my lap, and Erykah's melody.

"There is no mistaking that look in your eye. I saw it at the crap game, I saw it at the IHOP, I saw it in your car, I saw it up until you thought I didn't like your home." Her lips were smiling above the snifter, but in her eyes I saw the fear that I had heard earlier. I took a gulp and decided to redirect the mood. I wanted her, but I wanted her with her eyes wanting me.

"You're mistaken. If I were simply horny, you insulting my house would not change my mood. You're right; I am a Virgo, but what you saw in my eyes, I wouldn't call it horny."

"What would you call it?"

"Appreciation."

"For what?"

"Beauty. You're by far the most beautiful woman I've seen in a long time." I pulled her feet to my lips and kissed the tips of her toes. "And with that being the case, my dear, sweet, beautiful Sugar, I have to tell you good night before I make a fool of myself."

I stood and walked to the recliner across from the couch. I had shocked the sister, and it showed in the slightly confused expression on her face. I wasn't gonna leave her alone with the fear, but my company wouldn't cost her what she was willing to pay. I sat and made myself comfortable for a snooze. I couldn't leave her alone, but I couldn't sit with her dainty feet in my lap either. She didn't move from the couch.

"Three men have told me I was beautiful—my father, my husband, and you. It's such a strong word. I think black men are afraid to use it. I hear fine, gorgeous, built, foxy, damn good lookin', but seldom beautiful. Thank you, Mr. David Price . . . for everything. If you stay this sweet, I might make you mine." She motioned a toast in the air.

I didn't answer. I didn't want to talk to her. I know me. I would'a put it out of my mind that she was scared and needed my help. If I kept talking to her, eventually all I would see would be a beautiful, built, vulnerable woman in my house. I wanted to see and get to know more than that. Normally the recliner would have given me a comfortable snooze, but my 9mm's were digging into the small of my back. Past experience prevented me from unarming myself with a stranger in my home.

Romantically, my life had been a mess. I'd been in and

out of physical relationships quicker than a stray dog. I'd been divorced for over four years and had been intimate with more women than I cared to remember. In the beginning, it was great. Player, player back in the saddle, free to do whatever I wanted. But after the physical intimacy, I found myself still wanting. I combated the emotional wanting with more physical pleasure, five or six different women a month. It was crazy, but I didn't know what else to do.

I fell asleep listening to Sugar share the lead, quite well, with Erykah Badu on the song "Certainly."

Two

I woke later that day extremely well rested, which should not have been the case. I was expecting broken rest, caused by sleeping in the recliner with the 9 mm's in the small of my back. The chair actually slept quite well. I didn't open my eyes right away. The dream of my grandmama lingered. I could still smell the greens she cooked for my birthday. On my birthday, she would cook a pot of whatever I wanted, and it was all mine. I could share it if I wanted to, but I didn't have to share. I rarely shared the greens, the gumbo, or the black-eyed peas. I loved to eat, and my grandmama loved to feed me.

With eyes open, I realized I wasn't dreaming. The aroma of mustard and turnip greens opened my nose. My first thought was of Bonnie, my next door neighbor. She'd wrecked her husband Fred's new Ford truck a month ago and was still trying to make up. Bonnie was a damn good cook, but like a lot of working sisters, she only cooked on Sundays, and since it was only her and Fred, he didn't really pressure her. The one-day-a-week cooking was before she wrecked his truck. The scent of greens boiling, corn bread and lemon cakes baking, pot roast simmering, and catfish frying started creeping into my window the day the tow truck pulled Fred's wrecked F-250 into his driveway. Fred grumbled about that truck for days, but Bonnie stuffed him into silence. Every time he came out of the house, he was chewing on something. The insurance company replaced the truck, but I guess Bonnie kept cooking for good measure.

I settled back in the recliner, accepting my explanation for the aroma. I was about to close my eyes for a few more winks when I noticed all three of my pistols holstered and on the coffee table. I never left my firearms holstered if they weren't on my person, and I surely never left them on the coffee table. I hadn't drunk that much Remy. I woke up completely. One of the pillows from my bed was under my head and I was covered by the top sheet from my bed. I threw the sheet aside and stood. I inspected the pistols. They remained loaded.

I don't sleep hard. I've known women who could go in and out of my pockets pretty easily, but none that could disarm me without my knowledge. It just didn't happen. Sugar was crafty, much craftier than I'd given her credit for. That realization excited me.

It'd been awhile since a woman surprised me, showed me that there was more to her than I expected. I liked fast women, crafty women, experienced women, and the thought of Sugar being fast, crafty, experienced, and beautiful, got my jones rising. Nine times out of ten, a crafty woman was always a challenge. She had skills, which generally meant she could generate her own money, and an independent attitude came along with that. A woman can be crafty and as mentally slow as a sixteen-year-old in sixth grade. A fast woman thinks on her feet. Her mind, like the tiny red sponge ball in the three cap game hustlers play on the buses and the El-train, is quick and elusive. On the rare occasion when one is able to track the elusive red ball, the reward is great. At my age there was no substitute for an experienced woman. As my brother Charles once said, "I like to get to a party once it's started."

An experienced woman brought something to the table and knew her value. An experienced woman knew a man was only partially responsible for pleasing her. Just as a man was aware of his desires, so was she aware of hers.

Fast, crafty, experienced women aren't easily scared, but Sugar was. I left the weapons on the coffee table, stretched, and wiped the sleep from my eyes. It was time to get the whole scoop. I would shower and feed the dogs first. The scent of the greens was too strong to be coming from outside the house, but I didn't have any greens in the house, and there was no way Sugar got past Yin and Yang to leave for the store. The clock on the VCR read five PM. It was dinnertime for the Dobermans. No wonder I felt rested. I had slept for over nine hours. I heard Sugar humming in the kitchen. Not since my divorce had I awakened to a woman cooking and humming.

The first thing I noticed when I entered the kitchen were my two trained guard dogs. Yin, a two-year-old red Doberman, and Yang, a one-year-old black Doberman were both trained to kill. They sat sheepishly in front of the refrigerator. Neither would look me in the eye.

"What's going on here?" The question was more for the dogs than Sugar, and they knew it. The miserable mutts crept, heads lowered, behind Sugar for protection.

At first sight, Sugar was stunning. The early evening light passed through the kitchen window and over the sink to illuminate her like a picturesque Monica Stewart portrait in real life. She was standing over my grandmama's table, mixing what looked like cornbread batter in my grandmama's good mixing bowl with my grandmama's wooden mixing spoon. She had on one of grandmama's flowered sundresses, her house slippers (which used to be my granddaddy's), her apron, and my grandmama's scarf tied around her head.

When I asked my grandmama why she wore sundresses to work around the house, she said: "Your granddaddy loved me in these old flimsy thangs. At times I can still see him standing in the do' grinnin'. I wore 'em 'cause he loved me in 'em. I wear 'em now 'cause dey comfortable." If grandmama filled them dresses like Sugar filled this one, I know why grandaddy quit the railroad the moment he laid eyes on her.

"Now don't you come in here upsetting these puppies. If it wasn't for them, you wouldn't have this dinner going. *They* took me to the store while *you* slept." She was smiling. No, she was grinning. She saw the questions on my face, and it tickled her so much she was almost laughing. I spent a couple of seconds watching her breasts bounce as she mixed the cornbread batter. "Is that appreciation I see, Mr. Man?" I looked down to my dogs. They looked away. Apparently they were under the spell of Sugar's sweetness. I understood why they hadn't attacked her. They were trained not to attack people coming from inside the house, but the fondness they displayed was unprecedented. Ricky had known both of them since they were pups and neither would allow him to enter the house if he was alone. They certainly wouldn't allow him to roam freely through the house as Sugar obviously had done. I didn't risk commanding them to me, because of the embarrassment if they didn't heed my command. Now she was only grinning. I am sure their disobedience would have broken her out in laughter.

"You know those are killer guard dogs?" I asked, stepping farther into the kitchen.

"Really? That explains why people got out of our way when we walked to the store."

"You walked them without their leashes?"

"I could tell these boys didn't need a leash. Did you fellows?" Their stubs waved in response. "But they sure get attention. I like dogs. I've never had any as big as these, but there's not much difference. If they feel you like them, they like you."

She took the mixing bowl to the stove where she had a greased baking pan waiting. She poured the batter into the pan and slid it into the oven. Another pan that contained what looked and smelled like lamb chops was also in the oven. My mouth started watering, this was going to be a good meal. I decided not to ask about the guns.

"Did the dogs eat?" The mutts glanced up at me when they heard me ask about them.

"Oh yeah. They woke me up barking at the door. When I let them in they ran straight past me to their bowls, and looked up at me like I knew what to do. I found their food in the pantry and fed them. We've been friends since then. I found these clothes in the back bedroom. I hope you don't mind?"

"It's fine, baby."

"Do they belong to your ex-wife?" Her expression said she thought she already knew the answer. She thought she was being bold by wearing my ex's clothes.

"No, grandmama."

"Oh. We're the same size."

"Were. She died."

"Oh, I'm sorry. If I would'a known . . ." She cast her eyes down.

"It's OK. I didn't know what to do with her things. I'm glad you're getting some use out of them."

"Well, if you have any problem deciding what to do

with the mink stoles and muffs, you let me know. The same is true with the evening gowns and the rest of the sundresses. Your grandmama had exquisite taste."

"Thank you. I'm sure she would'a been flattered."

"Did she raise you?" she asked, stirring the simmering greens and adding chopped onions.

"No, but I spent a lot of time here. This was her house." I stood in the doorway of my own kitchen, uncertain of where to go.

"I saw the same baby picture on her dresser and yours. Is that you?"

"No. That was my son, Eric. He had a weak heart. He also died." I patted my thigh and my dogs came to me.

"I'm sorry, David."

"Yeah, me too." With some relief, I petted my dogs roughly.

"Do you have any other children?"

"No, just my two boys here. I do some work with the teenage boys in the neighborhood. That's their baseball equipment you saw in the front."

"Well, I hope you're hungry, because I cooked plenty and you bought the dinner. I put your change on your dresser upstairs." I passed on the opening to talk about her craftiness. "Oh, and David, a man came by and said he was your brother. He was in a bad way, so I gave him fifty dollars. I didn't want to wake you. If it's not OK, I'll give you the fifty back."

"No, that was fine. You're better than me. He would'a got me for a hundred or two."

"He's your older brother, huh?"

"Yeah, but not much older. The drugs have aged him. Look, I'ma hit the shower. I would tell you to make yourself at home, but you already have. Do me a favor and call Ricky. His number's on the speed dial. Push two. Find out what time he wants to meet." I kissed her lightly on the forehead and left her in the company of Yin and Yang.

Unlike Sugar, I was not able to go down memory lane with speed and a smile on my face. I missed my son and my grandmama. My brother was another touchy, emotional area for me. I was sure he did look in a bad way. I hadn't seen him in three weeks. He didn't like coming to me for money. I was his last resort. That was an agreement we came to years ago, me before crime. For Sugar to let him in the house and give him money without waking me, told me there was more to her than I guessed. Most people, black folks included, cringed at the sight of an addict in need. Why didn't Sugar?

She said the dogs woke her up, but I doubted it. Up close she looked like she hadn't gotten a moment's worth of sleep. Her face was tired, her eyes were strained, and the fear was still present. It was time to get the scoop, but I truly needed a shower. Actually, I needed all three Ss—a shit, a shower, and a shave.

Sugar made herself at home in my bathroom as well. Her sheer, pink panties and bra were drying on one of my wooden garment hangers, hanging from the shower rod. Her toothbrush was in my toothbrush holder, and her toiletries were on the shelf under my mirror. She'd even added her own brand of toothpaste. I must admit I liked the look of it. I liked the feeling of sharing my bathroom with her.

I had a job once as an assistant chemical compounder in a flavoring company. Basically, I was a laborer. I got to be friends with this Chinese guy named Phil. He believed Americans were filthy, that we didn't know how to clean ourselves. He said either we bathe and don't rinse, or simply rinse and don't bathe, which in my case was true. I either took a bath or a shower. I never took both. After he explained the logic of rinsing off the dirty water one bathed in, it made sense and became part of my normal routine. I bathe, and then I shower.

Sitting in the tub, I realized I should have called Ricky. I could have gotten info from him over the phone. I was slipping. Sugar had me slipping. She was getting close to me, becoming familiar. I didn't know enough about her to feel as familiar as I did. It was supposed to be the other way around. She was to develop a trust and familiarity for me. In a way, I guess she had. Her panties were hanging over my head.

What had me feeling uneasy was the subtle way she forced familiarity. She made herself at home as if she knew I wouldn't mind. She went in my pockets, spent my money, charmed my dogs, and didn't snub my brother. I didn't mind anything she had done, but again, I was uneasy because she knew I wouldn't mind.

As the hot water from the shower ran over the stubble that was growing from my bald head, I thought about how well Sugar filled grandmama's sundress. I switched the water to warm and began guessing what type of trouble she was in. I knew it was her husband, but I didn't know if he merely wanted her back, wanted her hurt, or wanted her dead. I offered protection and Ricky knew it, so it had to be more than him merely wanting her back. She said he had guns, no, she said they had guns. Who was *they*?

The towel I dried with smelled of lilacs. Sugar had dried with it. I liked that too. I plugged in my clippers and shaved my head and my face. I trimmed my mustache with a smaller, battery-operated set of clippers. I wiped the tiny bits of hair from the face bowl and walked nude to my bedroom, hoping Sugar may have found her way upstairs.

She hadn't. I threw my dirty clothes in the cleaner's

bag. I had no intention of putting on any drawers, but I decided to slow down and put some on, and jumped quickly into a Nike sweat suit. I rubbed on my sports deodorant and sprayed on a little Jazz cologne. I was thinking about the dinner, so I rushed and didn't lotion my skin. It was time for business.

When I walked into the kitchen, bare feet plopping on the tile, I first noticed Yin and Yang devouring a lamb chop apiece. Then I saw Sugar. She was slumped over my grandmama's table, sound asleep. I picked her up and carried her upstairs to my bed.

I had never tucked a woman in, but I tucked Sugar in. I fluffed up the pillows and watched her sleep for about twenty minutes. I wasn't really thinking about much of anything—wondering what she looked like as a baby, wondering how she would look when she turned seventy. I watched her. She slept hard once she went to sleep. She hadn't stirred once while I carried her up the stairs or laid her on the bed. I had almost tripped over my mutts leaving the room. Now both lay on the floor at the foot of the bed. They had made up their minds to protect her, and so had I.

I sat on the couch and checked the phone log to see if she'd called Ricky. She hadn't. I dialed his number. Her clutch was on the coffee table next to my guns. My normal action would have been to go through it. But just as I never went through my mother, grandmama, or ex-wife's purses, I didn't go through hers.

Ricky answered the phone on the first ring.

"What's up, D?"

I hate caller I.D. Carol told me all I had to do was dial *67 and my calls would not be identified, but I always forgot.

"You, Ricky. You the man."

"How's Sugar?"

"Sleeping like a baby."

"Man, you know she's family. I hope you didn't *rock* her to sleep."

"Naw, man. I wanted to, but like you said, she's family."

"You must be gettin' old, bro. That ain't never stopped you in the past."

Ricky was making reference to the brief affair between his younger sister and me. For years he'd gotten a guilty twinge out of me, but now I had the naming of his son David, and the scales were about to be even.

"She passed out after she cooked the meal."

"Did you eat any of it? Them Greer girls know how to cook."

"Not yet, but you know I am."

"What she cook?"

"Lamb chops, greens, cornbread, and fried corn."

"Damn! I'm on my way."

"What makes you think there's enough for you?"

"Look-a-here, you wouldn't've told me if it wasn't. I'll be there in ten." *Click.*

After I got off the phone, I immediately went into the kitchen and fixed my plate. Ricky is maybe a hundred or so pounds larger than I am, and he eats three times as much. Since childhood, I've had to get the jump on him at mealtime if I wanted my share.

Ricky was right; Sugar could cook. The food not only smelled as good as my grandmama's, but the taste brought back memories of her cooking. Sugar cooked with old school flair.

I was standing over the stove fixing my second bowl of greens, and spooning out another plate of fried corn and lamb chops when I saw Ricky pull into my backyard. He was moving so fast he barely closed the door to Martha's black Lexus coupe. He knew I was eating and trying to get full before he got to my house. Neither of us played when it came to good food. I watched him take the porch steps two at a time then stop suddenly when he remembered the dogs.

"D! You got them mutts? I don't want to have to bust a cap in their asses." He pulled his mama's .38 revolver from his belt as he looked around the yard. He wouldn't shoot my dogs, but he would shoot at them.

"They upstairs with Sugar," I yelled out the open window.

"Good, let me in. I know yo'greedy ass done ate up everythang."

I had to laugh. I hadn't, but I damn sho tried. It was enough left for him to get full and for Sugar to eat. I have had one friend outside of my brothers for most my life—Ricky. My father raised my brothers and me to be each other's friends. But even my daddy couldn't stop a friendship that death made.

I was in second grade with my brother Jackson, who had been kept back twice. Jackson was slow and everybody knew it. Everybody accepted it but my daddy. If I had a dollar for every time he told my mama, "Helen, if you treat the boy like he's slow, he'll be slow. Treat him like the others," I would be rich. My daddy was wrong. Jackson was slow. No matter how many whippings he got for peeing in the bed, he still did it. No matter how many times daddy slapped him for chewing his tongue, he chewed it. The ABC's remained a mystery his entire life.

My two older brothers and I protected him as much as possible. We washed the stained sheets during the nights and his soiled underwear during the days. We tried to keep wads of gum in his mouth, and when possible, took the blame for broken dishes and windows, and holes in the plasterboard.

Jackson would bang his head against the wall like he was trying to knock the confusion straight. He would spend hours watching ants, flies, butterflies, worms, or roaches. Bugs held his attention. We had to dump his pockets free of dead insects nightly in the summer. Daddy wanted him to be all right. But he wasn't, and we all knew it, including Jackson.

We all looked like our mama, except Jackson. He was the spitting image of my father, even down to the crossed left eye. My daddy came home the day before Jackson died and found him stuck in the living room wall. Jackson had pounded his head through the plaster and couldn't free himself. We thought daddy would kill him. When daddy took him out, Jackson was crying. Daddy held him like a baby, sat on the floor with him, and cried. That was the only time I ever saw my father cry.

Jackson was bigger than every kid in second grade and had three brothers who would kick anybody's ass who teased him. It wasn't the students who made school difficult for him; it was the teachers. It wasn't that they teased him, but they treated him special, and it pissed Jackson off. Despite my father's protests, they transferred him to an EMH (Educationally Mentally Handicapped) class. After his first day in the EMH class, he ran home from school by himself. We only lived a block and a half away, but we all went home together. We didn't know he left, so we were looking around the schoolyard for him when Ricky came and told us that a car hit Jackson. When we got home, it was over. The ambulance drivers had him covered with a sheet and were lifting him into the wagon. I tried to run to him, but Ricky held me back. He threw me to the ground and lay across me. He told me I didn't need to see him like that.

"He's broke, man, and you cain't fix him," he said.

Ricky said he then heard shots, but to this day, I don't

remember hearing them. Ricky rolled off of me and ran across the street to his house. I ran to the ambulance, but it pulled away. I was standing in the middle of the street yelling for my brother. Somebody grabbed me and hugged me tight. I thought it was my mother, but when I looked up it was Ricky's mother and her face was covered with blood. I fainted and banged my head real good on the concrete—my first concussion.

When I woke up in the hospital a day later, Ricky was sitting on my chest with a pillow over his head.

"You gonna tell on my mama?"

"What?"

"You gonna tell on my mama?"

"Get off of me!"

"I cain't. I knew you was gonna wake up today. You gonna tell on my mama? The police gonna take my mama. Dey said you saw her wit the gun. You gonna tell?"

"I ain't seen yo'mama with no gun. Get off of me." Ricky dropped the pillow and got off of me.

"If you tell dem you seen my mama wit a gun, dey gonna take her away," he said, sitting on the side of the hospital bed.

"I ain't seen yo'mama with no gun. Where is my mama?"

"Dey gone home. Da doctor told dem to leave. It's real late."

"Why you here?"

"My mama upstairs. I came down 'cause I knew you was gonna wake up. She shot my dad, den shot herself. I told dem I saw a man do it and he ran out da back. If you tell dem my mama had a gun, they gonna take her away."

"I ain't seen yo'mama with no gun. Get out of here."

"I cain't! If dey see me, I'll get in trouble. I got da gun."

"What gun?"

"I took it from her. If dey find it, dey gonna put her in jail."

"Get out."

"You got to keep da gun."

"I ain't."

"You got to. Dey ain't gonna look in yo'stuff for it. I cain't throw it away."

"You ain't got no gun."

"What's dis den?"

"You better throw it away."

"I cain't. Dey'll find it. It'll be me and yours if you keep it fo' me."

"Me and yours?"

"Both of ours."

"It's too big. I don't know where to put it."

"I do."

"Go ahead, but remember, it's ours."

I barely noticed Ricky's mother before the shooting. Hell, all I knew about Ricky was he couldn't fix or build anything. Whenever the chain on his bike slipped or it got a flat, he'd bring it across the street for me to fix. A big thing on our block was skateboards made out of two by fours and busted skates. Ricky couldn't make one roll to save his life. Having older brothers and a father who were always tinkering, I naturally developed a knack for fixing things.

Ricky's father came home when he felt like it, and the time he spent at their house was spent fighting with Ricky's mother. I seldom heard my father speak badly of any man, but he said Ricky's daddy wasn't worth the bullet that killed him. The neighbors on the block must have shared his sentiment, because no one came forward to challenge Ricky's story.

After the funerals (my brother's and Ricky's father's),

Ricky started hanging around our house. My mother kept inviting him and his sisters over to dinner. Their mother had to take on a part-time job, along with her full-time one to keep from losing their home. Ricky's mother didn't get home until eleven thirty PM, and my mother told my father that that was too long for Ricky and his sisters to be home by themselves. So after school, they came over to our house.

Having girls in the house everyday changed everybody. My mother busied herself showing and telling her borrowed daughters things my grandmama shared with her, things her sons showed no interest in. My father was less stern and hit none of us in the girls' presence. But he'd knock the hell out of us in front of Ricky, as if to let him know he was not exempt. My two older brothers lost their minds. They started showering, combing their hair, and putting on fresh clothes for dinner. If Ricky's two older sisters noticed, I couldn't tell, but his little sister sure did. She stuck behind my brothers like glue and hung on their every word. That left me, Ricky, and our gun.

It was three weeks after the funerals when Ricky's mother started asking us about the gun. She asked Ricky where it was. He told her he threw it in the lake. We lived on Sixty-second and Throop Street, miles from the lake. She slapped the shit out of him. Then she asked me where it was. I knew the lie was stupid, but I couldn't change it. I'd learned from lying with my brothers that one lie was easier. I said he threw it in the lake, and she slapped the shit out of me. She walked us to school the next morning, asked about the gun, and slapped us because our answer remained the same.

Ricky shared my bed that night when she came to pick him up. She woke me as well and again asked about the gun. Again we lied. She didn't slap us. She cried.

I begged Ricky to give her the gun. He said no because she might shoot somebody else. He started crying. I started crying. My mother came in the room and she cried, followed by Ricky's sisters and my brothers. We all sat in that room and cried. We cried for Jackson, and we cried for Ricky's daddy, who wasn't worth a bullet.

"Use your keys. I'm fixin' *another* plate."

"I ain't got my keys. I got Martha's keys. Open the do', nigga. I ain't playin!"

"Awright . . . damn, give a brother a minute." I smacked my lips as loud as I could out the window. "You wasn't lyin'; Sugar sho can cook."

"I'ma shoot this here lock off. Keep playin'."

Ricky barely uttered hello as he pushed past me, grabbed a plate, and headed to the stove. Yin and Yang entered, gave him their usual growl, and returned to Sugar. I sat at the table and finished my meal. We both ate in silence. I finished before Ricky, but I waited until he finished to ask him about Sugar. I wanted complete answers, and I wouldn't get them while he ate. He let go of his customary belch that signaled he was finished eating.

"Damn, she can cook just as good as Martha. You better try and get with her, D. Ain't too many women left that can burn like this."

"She's a married woman, brother. How am I supposed to get with her?"

"Look-a-here, that piece of nigga she got ain't shit. If he was worth something, she wouldn't be laid up under your roof, would she?"

I didn't answer right away. I wanted Ricky to tell me more. I went to the fridge and got four Samuel Adams lagers—two for me and two for Ricky. I sat back down and told Ricky to tell me about Sugar's husband.

"Why you gonna give me this here beer without an

opener?" Ricky stood and walked to the kitchen drawer. "You's a triflin' nigga," he said as he rifled through the drawer. He sat down, opened his beers, and tossed the opener on the table. "You didn't ask her about him?" he asked, looking at me sideways.

"Naw, I ain't ask her." I opened my beer, avoiding his glance.

"Why?"

"'Cause I ain't want to."

"You gonna have a married woman stay in your house and not ask about her husband? That don't sound like you, D." He was grinning. He knew he was on to something.

"You gonna tell me about him or what?" I was trying to be short with him, but my tone simply increased his grin.

"Don't get touchy, D, shit. I was just askin' why you didn't ask the married woman about her husband, damn."

Ricky's head was too big for the fingerwave hairstyle he wore. He hadn't changed his hairstyle since the seventies. A beige bowling ball with a finger-waved perm is what his head looked like to me.

"Who is he, Ricky?"

"Brother Yazz." He turned the Samuel Adams bottle straight up, draining half of it. I swear he was grinning and drinking at the same time.

"Brother Yazz? Brother Yazz of the New Day Brothers?"

"Yeah, that's the nigga."

I knew the look on Ricky's face all to well. He had that "I got your ass," that "I got you to do something you didn't want to do" look. Not a full smile, but a small, crooked, evil smirk.

"Man, what are you doing to me?"

"What?"

"Don't 'what' me, man! You pulling me into some of your mess!"

"Look-a-here, how you figga that?" he asked, restraining the smirk.

"Man, you and that brother been going at it for over a year. I ain't stupid." I drained my beer in three gulps.

"D, ain't nobody sayin' you stupid. My business is my business. I ain't involving you in my business. My wife's sister needed protection, so I sent her to you. This ain't got shit to do with my business. Your business is protecting folks, ain't it? She needs protection. That's what you do, at least that's what you say you do. I don't see how you make money protectin' niggas, but if that's what you say you do, I'ma look out fo' you and send you some business when I can. Shit, man, you should be happy I sent your ass some business, and I said I'd pay yo' fee. Damn, what else you want a brother to do?"

He said it all without taking a breath.

That confirmed it. Ricky always talked fast when he was trying to pull some mess. I had to admire him. He got me in smooth, and he'd covered shit with Sugar. A month ago he tried to hire me to do surveillance on Brother Yazz. I told him no and gave him Paul Phillips's card, a white private detective I've referred cases to in the past. Ricky said he didn't trust private detectives, but it was no problem because he would work it out. I should have known he wouldn't let it rest that easy.

"Man, you ain't right."

"I'm talkin' from the heart, D. This ain't got shit to do with my business."

"And you really think I'm going to believe that? Less than a month ago you tried to hire me to do surveillance on Brother Yazz. I told you then, the man was crazy. A crazy man with crazy followers. He's dangerous."

"You scared of him?" Challenge was in his hazel eyes.

"I ain't scared of no man. It ain't fear; it's common sense. A man with over seven hundred soldiers ain't a man to be messed with in no form, shape, or fashion."

"They ain't nothing but a gang. We dealt with gangs befo'."

"They ain't no gang, and you know it. If anything, they're a damn cult. He controls his followers' minds. They worship the man, and you know that shit."

"You gonna help Sugar or what?" he asked, trying to redirect.

"It ain't Sugar I'm helping, Ricky." I looked him straight in eyes until he lowered his. "Let's call a spade a spade. This is your mess."

"Look-a-here, I ain't the one needin' protection from him." He turned up his Sam.

"You the one who want him out your way. You the one want his soldiers off your weed-selling boys' backs. You the one that want them to stop raiding your swine-selling hot dog carts. You the one that want them to stop picketing in front of your liquor stores and organizing your slum tenants. You the one whose cleaning crews he convinced to strike for higher wages. This is yo'shit!" I didn't want to be angry, but I was getting there.

"Man, I got a right to do business like any other man in this country."

"Legitimate business," I snapped at him.

"My shit is legit!"

"Selling weed, crap games, slum tenements?"

"Look-a-here, ain't shit wrong with weed. It ain't crack. Shit, you smoked enough of it. I address the needs of the community: weed, liquor stores, and jobs. It's supply and demand, gotdamnit. As far as calling me a slum lord, where else these niggas gonna live for two hundred fifty dollars a month? Fuck, I ain't offerin' the Ritz. For two hundred fifty dollars you get four walls, heat, lights, and gas. Shit, the white folks downtown would'a closed me down if I was a slum lord. They didn't because I'm providin' adequate housin'."

"Would you live in one of your rooms?"

"I ain't no gotdamn crackhead. Who else gonna rent to them? I don't see the New Day Brothers offerin' cheap housin'. Shit, ain't nobody doin' it but me and the Jews, and I'm the only fool givin' 'em heat and lights with the rent. Shit, I barely made five thousand profit off that damn building last year. Yeah, I pay my cleaning crews seven dollars an hour, gotdamit. When I started the business I was lucky to come home with sixty dollars a week. I wish I could'a cleared seven dollars an hour. I didn't give a fuck about them niggas strikin', 'cause I knew I was payin' fair. If they didn't know it, there was plenty of niggas waitin' to cross that weak-ass picket line. Damn strike didn't last a day. Seven dollars is seven dollars.

"You know how hard it was for me and Martha and them damn kids in the beginnin', so why you talkin' to me like this? You know I been pickin' with the chickens since I was knee high, gotdamnit. Ain't nobody gave me shit. What I got, me and my baby earned, and I be shucked to shit if I let some fake Farrakhan nigga fuck with it!"

I didn't know if that was foam from the beer, or if Ricky was so mad he was foaming at the mouth. Either way, I decided not to say anything. I let my own anger cool. I simply opened my other beer and glanced out the kitchen window.

Ricky was right. Life hadn't been kind to him, and he made something out of nothing. We were in our third year of college, and Martha was in her first when she got pregnant. Abortion wasn't an option for either one, and Ricky was too proud for welfare. He dropped out and started mopping floors. It hurt me to see him do it, so I know it tore him up to actually do it, but he did it anyway.

"You gonna take the case, man?" he asked calmly.

"Yeah, I'll take the case, but my job is to protect Sugar. I ain't gathering a bit of information about Brother Yazz or his cult." I pointed my index finger at his chest to emphasize what I was saying.

"Cool . . . look, I'm outta here, man. When Sugar wakes up, y'all come by the house, OK? Martha wants to see her." Ricky pushed his three-hundred-pound plus frame from the table and stood up to leave.

"Hold up a minute, man." I asked to slow him down. "David—who did ya'll name him after?"

"Aw shit, Sugar done opened her damn mouth." He was grinning big time. He knew he was busted. I saw the dimples Martha claimed made her marry him.

"Man, that wasn't right. After all these years, to let me think you named that boy after me."

"I did name the boy after you. It wasn't my fault their daddy's name was David too. Damn, give me a break. As far as I'm concerned, the boy is named after you. Your name is David, his name is David." He was jingling Martha's keys in his hand, another nervous habit that told me he was bullshitting. "Don't sweat the lil' shit, my brother. Don't forget, soon as Sugar wakes up, y'all swing by."

If there was ever a man who was never caught, it was Ricky. My thirty-year friend squirmed out of more holes than any worm.

"We'll be there, man. Peace."

"Peace."

Whenever we argued, which was quite often, we always parted with "peace" to let each other know we were still cool, and ain't nothing serious going on. My daddy started us doing that after our first fight.

It started over a pair of gym shoes we stole from Kresgee's dime store. Neither of us needed the gym shoes. We didn't steal out of need. We stole for want. He stole one shoe and I stole the other. We fought about who was going to wear them first.

We were in the backyard trying to kill each other with belts and sticks. Daddy was in the garage with his buddies listening to Muddy Waters, playing Bid Whist, and drinking Old Grand-Dad. I don't know what brought him out of the garage, but he came out and lit into both our asses. He whipped Ricky like he was one of my brothers. After we finished crying, he made us sit in the garage and watch him and his friends drink, listen to the blues, and play Bid Whist. When his party was over, he called us both to him.

"Look, you boys might be friends forever, if you lucky. The fellows that just left here, I been knowing all my life. Two of them I went to Korea with, aces each one of them. We fight, but we stay friends, 'cause a black man needs his friends. Life is too short to be mad at a friend for any length of time.

"I'll tell you what me and old Johnny Ray do. We fought a lot when we were kids. Shit, we still fight, but when we leave each other, we always hug. It's our way of telling each other we still cool, despite the fight. You boys need to keep the peace between you. More than one friendship broke up because one buddy thought the other one was still mad. Shit, I know brothers that still don't talk to one another. Peace keeps people together. Now shake hands and hug, and tell each other peace."

And although we don't always hug, we always say "peace."

I had mixed emotions about Brother Yazz and his followers. On one hand, I admired the work he did for the community: the organized protests, the youth center, and the homeless shelter. On the other hand, I recognized him as a danger. Although the majority of his actions benefited the community, they all benefited him.

He managed to close down every liquor store on the south side except the ones he or Ricky owned. Brother Yazz justified owning his liquor stores because he didn't sell forty ounces of beer or cheap wine. He sold liquor and he also sold natural juices. He said he would only sell the liquor until he raised the consciousness of the community to the point where they would no longer need the white man's poison. Until that happened, he had no choice but to provide what was needed. But with every bottle sold, a customer got a pamphlet with Brother Yazz's seven steps to a better life. Step one being to stop drinking and using drugs.

I forked up the last few kernels of fried corn on my plate. Brother Yazz. Of all the men in the city, she was married to Brother Yazz. Brother Yazz controlled the minds of the people around him. He controlled their diets, their religious beliefs, and their bank accounts. I had never known of anyone leaving his organization. Supposedly, through him, one could find spiritual freedom and thereby receive all the blessings of the world.

He and his entourage drove around the city in Mercedes limousines. He dressed in pure white linen gowns, his followers in off-white. He spoke from both the Bible and the Koran. According to him, the truth was in both books, but only God's true servant could see that. I didn't know about that, but I knew how he got exposed to both books.

Brother Yazz's daddy was a storefront preacher from Fifty-first Street. He was shot dead by one of the widows in his congregation. At seventeen, Brother Yazz, then Raymond Owens, took over as pastor. With his mother's guidance, he moved the small storefront church into a new building in a little over five years. He was the talk of the town; a young preacher boy, barely out of high school, leading one of Chicago's largest south-side congregations. I don't know what happened, but soon after, he got arrested for bank robbery and served eight years. That nearly killed his proud mama. Raymond Owens came out of Statesville Penitentiary as Brother Yazz.

His followers, in the beginning, were mostly downtrodden people, people whom the community and society had turned their backs on—winos, the homeless, and crackheads. He and his mother opened a shelter the winter of his release, which provided him with a captive audience. It didn't take him long to build a following. The boy had charisma, the gift of gab, his daddy's good looks, and his mama's money.

Rumor had it that she closed the first church and sold the building without consulting any of the congregation. I don't know how much of that was true, but when you saw the woman, you didn't doubt any of it. She was high yellow with steel gray eyes and a face as stern as a repo man. She was one of those women who was always in the background, but you could tell she was running things. I would not only be protecting Sugar from Brother Yazz, but also from Brother Yazz's mama, and over seven hundred of his followers.

Sipping the beer, I wondered how much of a threat his mama really would be. After all, I wasn't aware that Brother Yazz was married. All I ever saw with him was his mama and his entourage. Maybe she wouldn't be a threat. Maybe she'd be happy Sugar was gone. I never knew a queen who was happy to share power.

The New Day Brothers were mostly an organization of men. The only woman ever seen traveling with the top dogs was Brother Yazz's mother. I was going to the fridge for another beer when Sugar's scream tore through me. I toppled the table running to her.

When I entered my bedroom, Sugar was sitting erect in the bed clutching one of my pillows. My mutts were on alert. Her scream disturbed them as much as it had disturbed me. Sugar's eyes were bucked wide open. She was sweating and trembling. I went to her, sat on the side of the bed, put my arm around her shoulder, and pulled her to me. I didn't ask her what was wrong. I only held her and let her cry.

"He's coming," she cried. "Brother Yazz is coming for me. I feel him! David, he's close and he's mad." She buried her head in my chest and sobbed. We sat there with her sobbing for a couple of minutes. I wanted to destroy whatever was making her cry. I told her it would be all right, that nothing or nobody was going to hurt her, and I meant it.

"You don't know him. He's not a normal man. He's got powers. He knows the insides of people, their thoughts, and their desires. He feeds off of them. He knew I was going to leave him, and that's why he started beating me. I'd be lying in the bed thinking of how to get away from him and he'd sit up and slap my face. He'd call me an ungrateful bitch and tell me I'd be dead before I was free of him. And I believed him." She pulled away from me and rocked herself. "I believed so much of his shit. I believed he was God's servant, God's gift to black people, the uplifter of our race. He pulled so many people from the gutter, me included. He was doing God's work. I saw it. He cleaned people of the slime of this world—addiction, prostitution, drinking, thieving—he washed it all from us. He cleaned us and made us new in God's light. He was God's servant, and we were his children, his disciples.

"We were to go into the world so others could witness his power. And we did it. People who knew us before couldn't believe the changes, so others came and we grew. He cleaned them all. It was God's work, truly miraculous. I'm talking about people like your brother, David, people in the world's grip, and he cleaned them. I saw it with my own eyes. People too nasty to ride a bus, now had jobs.

"When he asked me to marry him, I was honored . . . so honored. He knew what I was when I came to him. When I knocked on that shelter door it was the dead of winter, not only in season, but also in my life. I was wearing a pair of sweatpants that were so nasty they had to be soaked from my body. I had a hole in my crotch, which allowed a man to enter if he had a cocaine rock, ten dollars, or a warm place for me to stay. A year later I was cleansed through Brother Yazz's words and his readings. It was time for me to move from the shelter to one of the halfway houses. I was packing to leave when he proposed to me. He said I was shining brighter than any of his disciples, and God told him to make me his wife."

I didn't say a word. I sat and watched the tears flow from her eyes and listened to the words pour from her mouth. I wanted to comfort her, hold her, and tell her it was OK. But she was out of my reach, even though she was only an arm's length away. She needed to sit alone as she cried and talked.

"It was a beautiful ceremony. Only my New Day family was allowed. I understood because of the closeness of the disciples. Our holiest ceremonies are private. Outsiders, people who have not been cleansed by him, pollute the purity. I believed I loved him, and I believed God wanted us together. I had not been with a man since I walked through the shelter doors. The night of our joining he told me we had to wait until both of our blood tests came back negative. We spent the night praying to God.

"After the tests came back negative, he was fasting for God to bring more souls to be saved. He couldn't involve himself in any physical pleasure. After a year, I stopped expecting him to please me as a man pleases his woman. I was willing to make the sacrifice because he was more than a man. He was God's servant, or so I believed. I busied myself in readings and the workings of the New Day Brothers.

"God knows there was enough to do. We were growing so fast. Every week over ten people joined. My role changed. I was no longer there just to support him and bring new members. I was assigned classes to teach. That was a great honor. Only he, his mother, and Jamal taught classes. He assigned Jamal to teach me the principles that were to be taught to new members.

"Jamal and I got closer than either of us intended. Being heavily into the belief, we did what we were taught to do when temptations of the flesh grew strong. We went to Brother Yazz and asked for his guidance. I know it sounds stupid, but that's how our minds were working. We believed he was and knew everything. We believed he already knew of our unpure thoughts and would guide us back to purity. He did not offer guidance.

"He ordered Jamal to fast for three days and continue his teaching of the new members. He made me wear the filthy sweatpants I came to him in. He kept them, David. He kept them as tattered and smelly as they were the night I walked through the door. He handed them to me wrapped in pure white linen. When I unwrapped the package, I didn't remember them at first. He told me to strip and put them on. It wasn't seeing them that made me remember. It was the smell. I stood there in the prayer room, naked from the waist up, wearing the pants I forgot existed.

"He made me bend over and he entered the hole like hundreds of men before him. He called me every filthy name his mind could conceive. For three days, I stayed in the prayer room with a waste pot he forbid me to empty. He came into the room five or six times a day and went into the hole. 'Filthy bitch, skank ho, crackhead bitch, are what he called me while he tore into me. And after each time, he left a gift: diamond bracelets, earrings, broaches, gold necklaces, bundles of money, diamond rings, and all sorts of shit.

"It was his mother who released me on the third day. She came into the prayer room with two piles of clothes. One was worldly clothing, the other was an off-white, linen gown. She didn't say a word, just stood between the two piles of clothes. I wrapped everything he'd given me over the three days in those filthy pants. I slid into the gown and walked out with his mother.

"Whenever he came to my bed I wore those filthy pants and he paid well to enter the hole. His mother enrolled me in accounting classes at Harold Washington College. Tallying the ledgers became my responsibility. Can you believe it? In some sick sort of way, I had gained her trust. What was left of my faith, after those three days, disappeared once I started doing the books.

"It's all a scam. He and his mama are the main beneficiaries. Sure, everybody gets a cut, but nowhere close to what them two are hauling away. And the sickest part is that I'm still scared of him. I know he's not God's servant, but I still believe he's got power. The source just ain't God. The motherfucker is wicked. And I pray to God for the people I led to him.

"I don't want to just leave him, David." She looked into my eyes for the first time since she began talking. "I want to expose him. I want to bring the whole New Day scam down." She exhaled deeply. "You still want the case?"

Hell yeah, I still wanted the case. What man wouldn't? Bring him down? I wanted to end the bastard's miserable life. I wanted him to pay for each tear I watched drip from her eyes. What type of man taught faith and then took it away? I lowered my eyes because I didn't want Sugar to see the hate I felt. I didn't want her to misread what I couldn't hide. Ricky was right. Brother Yazz was a fake.

"Sugar, lie on back down and get some rest. Don't worry. I got your case."

"Are you sure?" I looked straight into those ebony stones encased in white marble.

"Yeah, baby, I'm sure." She rolled into my arms and gave me a tear-salted kiss.

"I told you if you stay this sweet I will make you mine." She cried, but she made me smile. "I don't need to rest, David. We got a lot of work to do. And Brother Yazz is close. I feel him."

Very little is accomplished when the mind is clouded with emotion, be it hate, love, or lust, and I knew this. That was why I took the dogs out to the backyard and wrestled with them while Sugar got dressed. I needed to clear my mind, and playing with them usually helped. But neither the mutts nor I were into it. We all kept looking back toward the house for Sugar. I sat on the porch steps and let them run back into the house to her.

I have a custom made holster which allows me to wear two 9 mm's in the small of my back. I also keep a .22 caliber automatic pistol strapped to my ankle. I've yet to fire either while working on a case.

Sugar said she'd seen the New Day Brothers' guns. The thought of an armed cult didn't rest easy with me.

The evening sky was beautiful. The sun was setting and burnt orange claimed the sky. I've seen pictures of other parts of the country: desert sunsets, ocean sunsets, and they all look beautiful. But I ain't never seen them in real life and doubt they were any more beautiful than the ones that grace my city. True, we may not have mountains, but I never saw a skyline more colorful and proud as ours.

Sugar had a plan and she needed me to protect her while she worked it out. This wasn't my usual role. Usually I led and others followed. When a celebrity came to town, his or her personal bodyguards trusted my judgment concerning the safest routes, and the safest entry and exit points to any destination. I was rarely second guessed. When a wife was trying to escape an abusive husband, she followed my directions and she stayed safe. When a gang member was being sought, he did what I said, and he lived. I'd never had a client hurt under my protection, but I'd never followed a client's plan either.

This case was going to be different. Sugar not only needed protection, she needed protection while she was being an active threat to an organization of nuts: people who believed God was on their side, people who followed a man who relieved them of burdens; a man whom they felt was God-sent.

Whatever Sugar's plan, it had to be executed quickly. We were outnumbered and outgunned. Of the five security escorts working under me, none were qualified for this. My daddy's words entered my mind: "A black man needs his friends."

"You ready, David?" Sugar called to me softly through the screen of the back door. She was dressed in her own clothes. The black dress was just as stunning as ever.

Was I ready? I wasn't sure. But I was sure I wasn't going to let anyone hurt Sugar.

Three

On the ride to Ricky's, I really wasn't in the mood for talking. That didn't stop Sugar. I tried to give her short, quick answers, hoping she'd get the hint. But if she did, she didn't act like it. I needed time to think, and her constant questions wouldn't allow me to hold a thought.

"So how did you get into this business, David?" I couldn't think of a short answer for that question, so I gave her a long one.

"I didn't have a job. The hospital I was working at laid me off, and to be truthful, I was tired of the profession."

"What were you?"

"A mental health counselor. I graduated from Circle, excuse me, UIC nowadays, with a degree in psychology. I worked for ten years, and I was simply tired of it." I thought about turning on the radio to distract her questions.

"Counseling, mmph. That seems like it would be so rewarding. Why did you get tired of it?"

I thought about being blunt and telling her I really didn't

want to talk, but I decided against it and answered her question.

"In the beginning, I felt like I was making a difference. After a while it became apparent that with only a bachelor's degree, I would never be more than an enforcer."

The scent of lilacs surrounded Sugar. It wasn't really hot enough to have the air on, but the climate control in the Fleetwood had the air crisp and comfortable. Climate control impressed some women.

"Enforcer?"

"Yeah, that's how I felt. It was my job to make sure the patients took their medication and followed treatment plans the doctors and social workers designed. I had some input in treatment plans, but my advice was rarely taken seriously. For the most part, the doctors were foreigners, Asians mostly. They were people who were culturally unaware of the stressors of American life, and even less aware of the stress a black person goes through. I got tired of my suggestions being ignored, and I got tired of forcing medication I didn't believe in on my people.

"The medicine stopped hallucinations, but it also robbed people of their spirit, their essence. I knew patients who had hallucinations all day, but they were able to play chess, card games, and interact on a conscious level. Not true after the medicine got into their systems. They would sit for hours not responding to anything. The medicine didn't affect all the patients like that. A lot got better, but the majority I worked with didn't.

"I got overwhelmed by the attitude of the doctors. If the patients weren't violent and were not having hallucinations, they were fine. I wanted more, but nobody cared about what I wanted. My job was to make sure medicine went down the patients' throats. I didn't have enough faith in the system to go back to school and further my education. I didn't think it would do any good. I was one man against a system. I became discouraged and apathetic about my work. When the layoff came, I didn't care." I nearly ran the light at Sixty-third and Stony Island, talking.

"You know, you were wrong."

"Maybe." I made a right onto Stony Island. Ricky lived on Sixty-eighth and South Shore Drive.

"No, you were. One person can make a difference." She wasn't talking about me quitting my job. The determination in her face was for herself.

"I didn't have the fight in me. And besides, I was tired of working for others, taking orders from people no smarter than me, people with more education, but less common sense and compassion. And I was getting jealous of Ricky. He was doing his own thing and making a lot of money." I drove past the YMCA and remembered my membership was past due.

"You two are a strange pair of friends. He says similar things about you."

"Really, like what?" I couldn't think of anything Ricky would envy about my life. He had six smart and talented kids, several successful businesses, and a wife who allowed him to be himself.

"Never mind. We're talking about you. How did you get started in this business?"

"Well, like I said, I was laid off so I was drawing unemployment while deciding what to do with my life. I knew I wanted to be my own boss, but I didn't know what of.

"Anyway, I was living in Harvey at the time. And, like I said, I was getting unemployment. I cashed my checks at the local currency exchange. At the currency exchange I began noticing all these old people cashing their monthly checks. Once they cashed them, they became edgy, nervous, and paranoid, and for good reason. The majority would have to walk across the street and wait for the Pace bus. There they became vulnerable to the casualties of poverty. Young men with nothing preyed on old folks with little. The first time I saw three young boys beat an old man to the ground and take his money, I knew I had to do something.

"It started out as a senior transportation service, picking up old folks on check days and taking them around, and making sure they got home safe. It wasn't supposed to be a business. It was just something I was doing. Then one day this gang, a group of about five boys, tried to rob the old folks I was walking to the car. I got so pissed off, I ignored the gun one of them held and tore into their asses. To make a long story short, one of the boys got shot in the head and died.

"I didn't shoot the kid, but I still had to go to court about it. The judge dismissed the charges, but she told me if I planned to continue operating a bodyguard service, I would have to be licensed. I didn't know I had a bodyguard service. She lit a light for me. But when I went to the state building to register the business, I was told I couldn't operate a bodyguard service in Illinois. I could have a security service. So I went to security school, got my license, and started my security escort service."

There was more to the story, but that was all I was willing to tell Sugar at the time. If we were going to talk, which was obvious, I wanted to hear about her plan. How was she planning to expose Brother Yazz? Exactly how many followers did he have? Did she have information? Was it written or on tape? Could the information be used in court? What was she planning?

"Why did you get divorced?" she asked.

Now that was a loaded question, one I hadn't completely answered for myself. There was no way I was going down that path.

"Sugar, let's talk about your plan, OK?"

"Touchy area for you?"

"Yes and no. But what's important right now is your safety, and that depends greatly on what you have planned. So let's talk about that." I made the left at Sixty-seventh, cutting through Jackson Park.

"I know. I wasn't trying not to talk about it, but what I'm involving you in is dangerous. I'll never forgive myself if you're hurt."

"I'm a big boy, Sugar, and I've been taking care of myself for a while."

"OK." She looked away from me. "My plan revolves around the ledgers. I hid a copy in the prayer room. The morning I left I was too hurried to get it."

"When did you leave?"

"Thursday morning."

"And you think they're still there?"

"Yes. He has no reason to think I made a copy. He was only concerned with me leaving. The egotistical bastard couldn't conceive of me having a brain, never mind wanting revenge. The ledgers are there."

"What about his mother?"

"I don't know, David. That woman is still a mystery to me. I don't think she suspected anything, and even if she did, she would never find where I hid them. No one suspects a thing, I'm certain."

"What about Jamal?"

"I have to save him, David. I've got to open his eyes. He's such a sweet man."

"He doesn't know?"

"No. We stopped talking after we confessed our feelings to Brother Yazz."

"Do you still have feelings for him?" I had to ask.

"No. I needed a friend, someone to pay me some attention. I was a new bride and my husband treated me like a servant. I feel pity for Jamal. He believes in a man who is not real, a man who is a fraud, a hustler, a false prophet, a demon, a motherfuckin' trickster."

What I saw in Sugar's eyes when she spoke of Brother Yazz made my skin crawl. It was a look I'd seen on only one other woman's face. I saw it on Carol's face when she was trying to run down her then husband with their Dodge Caravan. She would have succeeded if I hadn't jumped in the way. It was the look of a scorned woman who was fed up.

"How do you plan on getting the ledgers back?"

Sugar's tight face and narrowed eyes told me she had more planned than retrieving the ledgers. Part of me was down for it, whatever it was. Part of me knew exposing the New Day organization would be enough, but the part that was down with Sugar's scorned face wanted whatever she wanted.

She didn't answer my question right away. Her face was almost knotted. It wasn't until she noticed that we were in front of Ricky's house that her face relaxed.

"I'll tell you that once we go in and settle down." Her tone was final, and I didn't want to push her. Her face said she was not to be pushed. I parked my Fleetwood behind Ricky's Ford Expedition.

Ricky's home could be called nothing less than a castle. It looked like a castle—a small castle, but a castle nonetheless, complete with steeple, those ugly gargoyles on the roof, and huge gray stone blocks that made up the body. Each step leading to his front door was close to eighteen inches high. A wrought iron gate provided a barricade four feet in front of an iron-studded, oak door.

Admiration did not express how I felt about Ricky's

home. Neither did envy, because I wouldn't want to live in it. Appreciation came close. There were only two structures on Ricky's block—a large court-way building made from beige stone, and his castle. Across South Shore Drive, east of Ricky's home, was the South Shore Country Club and Lake Michigan. I'd woken up many mornings in Ricky's front room, and I knew the sun shone on his home first. Every inch of his living room was blessed with the morning sun.

Saturday evenings at Ricky's home very seldom changed. I expected to walk in and hear a television going, a radio or CD player playing, his ten-year-old twins, Monique and Monica, arguing, Martha in the kitchen fussing with their oldest daughter, Tiffany, about her lack of attention to what Martha was trying to teach her about cooking, and Ricky complaining about his boys, Mark and Anthony, cheating him at Nintendo. And that was pretty much what I heard when I let Sugar and myself in.

Martha was baking, and my nose told me it was caramel cake. All the tightness left Sugar's face as Saturday evening at Ricky's pushed Brother Yazz from her immediate thoughts.

"Hey y'all!" she called into the house. She cheerfully glided through Ricky's enormous living room into what should have been his even larger dining area.

The dining room remained large, but Ricky and Martha seldom used it for formal dining. It was their family room. The kids' homework was done there, Nintendo was played there, television was watched there, and the whole family lounged there. There was no dining room table in the room. Instead, the room held two Acer computers, two Sony televisions (one big screen and one smaller nineteen-inch for the Nintendo), two of those big corduroy couches, and three or four futons.

"Auntee Sugar!" the twins screamed from one of the

futons. "Auntee Sugar is here, Mommie!" They ran to her with ponytails flying and gave her an embrace that only loving children could give. "Hey Auntee," the boys said. They did not rise from the couch or take their eyes from the battling karate warriors on the smaller Sony.

They shared one Nintendo controller while Ricky held the other, battling against both of his sons. On the big screen *The Preacher's Wife* was playing, and the volume was turned up loud, I guessed so Martha could hear it in the kitchen. I knew Ricky wasn't watching it. Nobody had said hi to me yet. I wanted some little girl hugs too.

"Y'all don't see nobody but yo' Auntee Sugar?" I asked the twins.

The girls looked at me and said hi, but they weren't leaving Sugar's embrace. Neither the boys nor Ricky broke their gaze to say anything to me. I walked though the family room into the kitchen, hoping to fare better in there.

"Hey, Uncle David," Tiffany said.

"Hey, sweetness. Your mama got you in here working like a Hebrew slave, huh?"

"A what?" Her face, which fortunately favored Martha's more than Ricky's, told me she'd never heard that saying before. "I'm not sure what you're saying, Unc, but if you're asking if Mama is working my fingers to the bone, the answer is yes." Like always, her smiling, round face was a pleasure to see. Her head was full of big, black curls. Ricky made her take out the huge braids she had last time I saw her, and I was pleased. She looked more like a little girl with the curls, and I was in no hurry for her to grow up.

"Child, hush. That li'l bit of batter you mixed ain't gon' hurtcha. Hey, D! You and my sister spent the night together, huh?" It was merely a question, but what I saw in her eyes made me want to spill every emotion I thought about feeling for Sugar. This woman wanted her husband's best friend married, and not for her own selfish reasons. She knew my divorce had not influenced Ricky. Ricky did what he wanted, and she'd grown to accept it without blaming others.

When I got divorced, I don't know who was hurt worse, me, my wife, or this round-faced, brown-skinned, short, brick house, sanctified sister before me. She believed I needed a mate and never hesitated to tell me so. She described me as a giving soul, and, according to her, giving souls needed somebody close to give to, or the world would take advantage of them. I saw questions in her eyes, she was wondering if her sister had what I was looking for.

I never went out with any of the sanctified church sisters she tried to hook me up with for one reason: I didn't want God mad at me for dogging one of his lambs. After my divorce, I was in dog mode, and I told her that.

"Well one thing for sure, D, you ain't got to worry about hurting that one. You better watch yourself around her. She's my baby sister, true enough, but I ain't never known her to miss a beat over a man, not even that heathen snake she supposed to be runnin' from now. I love her, D, but you be careful with her. She and Ricky got a lot in common, you know what I mean?" I didn't, but I smiled and said I did. I tossed my keys on the table and sat down.

"Tiffany, you go on out there with the rest of them, and close the door behind you. Me and your uncle got something to talk about."

"Ma! I'm supposed to be making the cake for Daddy." Her words protested, but she was already taking off the apron and moving for the door. It was obvious Tiffany didn't enjoy the cooking or the cooking lessons Martha gave her.

"Child, I had to almost beg you to come in here. Don't worry, we'll tell your daddy you baked him his cake."

"Thanks, Ma," she said, smiling while she pulled the door closed.

"That child cares as much about cookin' as a poodle does a fish. Her mind ain't on nothin' but them music videos and clothes. How she gets As and Bs in school, only the Lord knows, 'cause she don't pay attention to nothing around here."

"How old is she now?" I asked, peeping into the mixing bowl on the table. "Twelve?"

"Fourteen goin' on thirty," Martha answered, smiling and shaking her head like my mother used to do when she was signifying on one of us. I stuck my finger in the mixing bowl, wiping up some of the leftover batter. Martha sat across from me.

"David, I want you to be careful with Sugar." Again she put me in mind of my mother. Her eyes were those of a mother, warning a hardheaded child that she knew wouldn't listen. "She's not a bad person. Selfish, yes, but it ain't all her fault. Men have spoiled her, and my daddy was the worst.

"Sugar ain't my blood sister. Mama and Daddy went downtown one day and came home with her. I was eight, and she was six. From the day she came home, I shared everything I had with her, but it wasn't enough. She wanted her own stuff, and Daddy gave it to her. Mama and Daddy tried to make up for whatever bad thing happened to her before she came to us, but they couldn't. They gave her their name, a home, and a good education. Everything they gave me, they gave her, but nobody but Sugar can come to grips with her past.

"You know our folks wasn't rich. Daddy had his body shop, and Mama worked as a clerk for the city. When those boys broke in the house and killed them, we weren't left with much. But we split it all down the middle—the sale of the house, the shop, and the insurance. After the funeral and all the business of death was over, we split up. I was twenty, and she was eighteen. We both got our own apartments and went to different schools. I went to Circle, and she went to the Art Institute. She did well on her own, graduated, and started her own interior design business. I was really proud of her.

"After David was born and me and Ricky was planning our wedding, I got in touch with her and asked her to be a bridesmaid. She said yes. She came to the rehearsals and everything, but she didn't show up on my wedding day. You were just the opposite—didn't make one rehearsal, but came to the wedding." She smiled at me, teasing.

"She never called to apologize or anything. She moved out to Los Angeles. I hadn't heard from her for years, since David was a baby. Then about five years ago, I was doing Ricky's personal books, and I saw checks written out to her. They weren't small checks either—a thousand dollars here and two thousand there. I seldom ask Ricky about his personal business, but I asked him about them checks!

"I guess writing checks, instead of wiring her money, was his way of tellin' me about her. He told me she wasn't doing too good out in California. I asked him why he didn't tell me about it, and he said she asked him not to. She thought I was still angry about the wedding. Which I was, but she was family. I told Ricky to tell her to come home if she was in trouble. And, I told him if he sent her another check, his bighead butt would be moving to California with her.

"A month or so later, I let Ricky send her a plane ticket and we picked her up at the airport. When I laid my eyes on her I knew she was in trouble, and I knew it was drugs. All her weight was gone, her skin was dry as sand, and her eyes were dull. My baby sister got off that plane with all her belongings in one lil plastic bag. One thing I know about drug addicts, David, from working in the hospital, is you cain't help them if they don't want to be helped.

"She stayed with us about four months. I didn't mention drugs or any treatment programs. I fed her, bought her some new clothes, and didn't pressure her about anything. I gave her time to pull her life back together. You know this place got a million rooms, so her staying here was no problem."

I had done similar things for my brother, so it didn't surprise me that Martha would show such love.

"She never went out those first couple of months. She stayed in, kept the twins, cleaned the house, and cooked. Around the third month, she started to get a lil' antsy. Ricky hired her to decorate the house and, D, that did it. She was back to her old self, justa fussin', snobbin' folks, and going out to shop for furniture and paint. Working brought her back.

"Ricky recommended her to a couple of folks whose businesses he cleaned, and she got a lil' clientele going. Sugar and I didn't talk much while she stayed here. We talked around each other. After she got back to her old self and got a lil' money coming in, she moved, but there were no hard feelings about it. Ricky and I both felt it was our job to help her get back on her feet. Once on them, she was on her own. When she first moved, she stayed in touch, came over on Saturday nights, babysat the twins, took Tiffany shopping, and the boys to Sox and Bulls games. She was a regular aunt.

"Since we never really talked, I don't know what started her back to smoking that stuff. But gettin' high doesn't go with being an aunt or a sister, so she faded out of our lives again. Ricky tried to find her, but he couldn't. I hadn't seen her until she showed up here Thursday night. I think Ricky found out she was with them New Day fools, but he didn't tell me.

"Nothing would make me happier than you two getting together. But make sure it's you wanting her, and not her making you want her. There's a difference, D, and you men like to act like there ain't. Be sure you know what you're doing with her." Martha got up, went to the stove, and checked the boiling milk and brown sugar. "Be sure, David."

"What makes you think I might have feelings that serious?" She turned from the stove and looked me straight in the eyes.

"I know Sugar, and I know you. You like to give, and she likes to take. And you need somebody right now, even if you telling yourself you don't. Four years is a long time for a man like you to be alone."

"I haven't been alone," I said in a mack-daddy tone.

"Tell me the name of the last woman you slept with."

"Uuhhh . . . uuhhh." Damn, I couldn't think of one name.

"You been alone. Hand me that vanilla on the table." I picked up the vanilla and walked over to her. "Shoot, D, if you and her really got together, it would be marvelous. I know you thinking about it, or else you wouldn't come in here to talk to me. You would've been sittin' out there with the rest of the boys playing war on the television. You miss having a family. I didn't think you would ever get over Eric. I saw a part of you die with your son, and I saw another part die with the divorce." I backed up from her and sat back down.

Martha had never talked about my son's death with me before. All she offered was, "It's God's will."

"He was such a beautiful boy," she said. "Seems like that smile never left his face. I cain't think about him without thinking about your grandmama. I never saw him without her. She all but took him from you and Regina.

"When he died, I prayed that you wouldn't take his death out on your marriage. Y'all were so happy before he died. The death of a child changes so much. Your grandma died what, a month later? You ever think about what you went through that year, D? You lost your son, your grandmama, and your wife. And you try to act like nothin' happened. You need to stop and take a breath, baby. It's time to take time, time to think, time to feel. I could be wrong, but that's how it looks to me.

"Your son dies, your grandma dies, you leave your wife, you quit your job—no, your career, what you went to school for. And I know you quit, David, because I worked for the same hospital. You go back to school to be a bodyguard, a security guard. What did they say at that school when you told them you already had a bachelor's degree?

"I don't know all the details between you and Regina, and I ain't laid eyes on her in over three years. But she calls me once a month to see how you doing. She usually makes me promise not to tell, but one time she forgot. She was babysitting or something, and the little boy rushed her off the phone. You got unfinished business hanging all around you, D, and you won't slow down to deal with it. You just keep going, working, building your business, hanging out in the streets, jumping in and out bed with all types of women. Take time to feel, D. Get a grip on your past before it ruins your future."

She was hitting home too hard and too fast, and I wanted out of the kitchen.

"You ain't no spring chicken, boy. You too old to have heavy burdens on your back, burdens that time and Jesus will take from you. I know you don't like talking about Jesus, and I also know you ain't been to church since Eric died. But Jesus heals, David. Working yourself stupid won't heal you, and running the streets won't heal you. Slow down, David, and call on Jesus. He'll come." She bent and kissed me on my cheek. I didn't know I was crying until I felt her lips on me. I stood up and left the kitchen.

I walked quickly through the family room to the front closet. I went into Ricky's coat pocket, pulled out his cigarette case and lighter and went outside into the night air. I sat on his top step and lit one of his joints.

Almost ten months had passed since I last smoked a joint. It had become a part of my daily routine after my divorce. I had a joint with my morning cup of coffee, a joint before and after sex, a joint after dinner, and a joint when I took a dump. I stopped when I noticed fat cells growing behind my nipples. Getting high wasn't worth having titties.

I sat there smoking and wondered why I should stop to feel when what I felt hurt. In four years, I built a very successful business that employed seven people, including myself. I remodeled my grandmama's house. I bought myself a new Caddy. I wasn't doing too badly. I inhaled the smoke deeply. I did need a break. Maybe after this case I'd take a trip down to Arizona and visit the folks. I hadn't seen them since the Christmas after grandmama's funeral.

Ricky's voice interrupted my thoughts.

"What, you spend time in the kitchen talking to my saint, then you run out here and smoke my devil's weed? You a strange brother, D. Pass me the joint," Ricky said and eased out onto the porch.

"Fuck you. Here." I passed him the joint. He sat next to me on the step.

"I thought you was finished smokin' this shit. You said it had you growing titties."

"I thought you minded your own business."

"Look-a-here, nigga, this my weed you smokin' on, so it is my business."

I went into his cigarette case, pulled out another one of his joints, and lit it.

"Damn, nigga! Them ain't no Newports. This some of California's finest Sensy. This shit ain't fallin' off the trees around here. Look-a-here now, make that cha last one. Damn! What the saint say to you?"

I didn't answer the question, so neither of us spoke. We sat silently inhaling the smoke from California's finest Sensy. He passed me the bottle of Remy he was holding in his other hand. I know Remy is meant for sipping, but I gulped.

"Damn," Ricky said as he turned his eyes to look at me without turning his head. I could tell he wanted to reach for the bottle, but he changed his mind. When he finished his joint, he picked up his gold cigarette case from the step and opened it. He had two joints left. I looked away when he turned to see if I was watching him. He pulled both from the case and handed me one. He snatched the Remy back.

"You ever tell Martha about them dudes?" I asked, talking about the boys that killed Martha's parents.

"What dudes?"

"You know the ones I'm talking about."

"Naw, ain't never had no reason to."

"She talked about it a little tonight."

"She asked about the dudes?"

"No, she was talking about her parents dying."

"Sugar put her in mind of that. You know how it is. You see one of yo' family, you start thinkin' 'bout the rest of 'em."

"Let me get a little more of that Remy."

"You didn't bring no drank wid'cha?"

"Naw."

"Damn, nigga you's triflin'. I bet you gon' want some of my cake, too, ain't cha?"

"You got that right."

"What cha think 'bout Sugar?"

"She's fine."

"Yeah, but she ain't as pretty as Gina."

"What's with you and Martha tonight, bringing up Regina? She coming over here or something?"

"Naw. Damn, I just said Sugar wasn't as pretty as her."

"Regina is pretty, but Sugar is fine. There's a difference."

"So what's the difference between fine and pretty?"

"Women are born pretty. They have to work on being fine. You had enough to drink. Give me that bottle."

He pulled the bottle out of my reach. "Shiiit, liquor store up the street, nigga, right across them tracks. It's one of Brother Yazz's stores, and usually I wouldn't spend a dime in the place, but it's the closest one around here."

"Well, I ain't gonna drive after smoking that stuff. Walk with me."

"What?"

"Come on," I said, standing.

"Nigga, do I look like I walk anywhere?"

"Nope."

"What cha sayin?"

"I just answered your question, bro."

"Oh, I can walk up there!"

"I don't doubt it, brother."

"Fuck you and them damn fat jokes."

"Ain't nobody making no fat jokes, man."

"Hold on, let me get my roscoe out the closet."

While walking the four blocks to the store, I regretted

prodding my best friend into the walk. Hearing his laboring breath, I realized how obese he'd become. Just as the guilt was really kicking in, we entered the store, and his breathing became almost normal. His eyes lit up when he saw the snack stand. I must admit, I got a little excited too. It was a Hostess stand loaded with fruit pies, Twinkies, honey buns, and shortcakes.

We were both filling our arms when a voice interrupted us from behind.

"Well good evening, Brother Brown. It's good to see you shopping with us. The Lord is good."

I didn't bother to turn around. I figured it was someone from Martha's church who knew Ricky. I carried my goodies to the counter and ordered a bottle of Remy.

"Son of a bitch! I don't know your Lord," Ricky said.

I turned and saw he'd dropped his arm full of goodies on the floor and was standing face to face with Brother Yazz.

"And motherfucker, if you lay yo' hand on me again, I'll kill ya!" I guessed Brother Yazz had touched Ricky's shoulder from the back when he approached.

"Brother Brown, why such a hostile greeting?" Brother Yazz placed his open palms on his own chest. He was dressed in pure white linens, his jet-black hair was waved to the back, and he stood as tall as Ricky. That surprised me. I always thought of him as a short man.

"Nigga, you ain't seen hostile if you don't get the fuck outta my face." Three of Brother Yazz's followers walked up behind him. It was reflex more than anything else, but I drew both 9 mm's from my back and let go of two rounds. The three followers hit the floor, but Brother Yazz and Ricky remained locked in a hateful gaze.

"You need to control your dog a little better, Brother Brown. There was no need to fire a gun in my establishment."

"Nigga, consider yourself lucky he didn't put a slug in yo' pretty ass."

"Let's go, Ricky!" I called from the door. When we got outside, Sugar had my Fleetwood door open and waiting.

"I felt you, baby!" she said as we peeled from the curb. "I told you, you were mine!"

"Damn, D, why ya wastin' bullets like that? You shoulda shot that nigga! I was ready to put a cap in his ass if one of his boys would'a flinched. Motherfucker had the audacity to put his slimy ass hands on me. And the bastard knows I cain't stand the ground he walks on. Son of a bitch! Sugar, you think he saw you?"

"I don't know."

"What made you come up here?"

"I felt David."

"What cha talkin' 'bout, girl?"

"I knew he was in trouble."

"Why you feelin' that nigga? You didn't feel nothin' 'bout me?"

"No."

"Ain't that some shit? I'm your brother-in-law. You should be feelin' me."

"I'll leave feeling you to Martha, OK?"

I sat in the backseat of my own car looking at the 9 mm's that remained in my hands. What was it about being around Ricky that caused me to fire pistols? The only time I ever shot a pistol, other than on the range, was when I was in his company. I looked out the back window to see if we were being followed. We weren't. Brother Yazz must not have spotted Sugar. Ricky's cellular phone rang.

"Hey, Martha. We OK, baby. Your sister just got a little excited. We gonna stop by The Other Place and have a drink before we come in. Yeah, they spendin' the night.

Yeah, they know they cain't sleep together in a Christian house. I love you, too. See ya in a lil' while." He put the phone back in his pants pocket. "Well, no oochie coochie fo' y'all tonight. The saint done laid down the law!" I holstered my pistols as we all laughed a much needed laugh.

Ricky and I enjoy hanging out at The Other Place for different reasons. My reasons were the live jazz and the fact that they served Remy Martin V.S.O.P. Ricky's reason was that married women frequented the club. According to him, there was no better person for a married man to cheat with than a married woman. Nine times out of ten, she ain't looking to leave home and neither is he. And married women, again according to Ricky, are usually disease free, so he didn't have to wear a rubber. I couldn't believe a married woman having an affair would not insist upon a condom, but according to Ricky, when they found out he was married, they were OK with no condom. I tried to stay away from married women, mostly because I was a married man who caught his wife cheating. I figured if I caught mine, another husband could catch his, and I didn't want to be on the other side of the kicked-in door.

I wasn't sure if the weed was kicking back in or what, but once I walked into The Other Place, I instantly felt mellow. I'm talking that deep down mellow, that slow-walking, smooth-talking, jazz-listening mellow. The band was just setting up, and the place was only half-full. We grabbed a table in front of the stage. The waitress didn't even ask. She brought us three Remys as soon as we sat down.

"OK, which one of you is the regular?" Sugar asked in response to the unordered drinks. Ricky winked, stood, and said he saw an old friend at the bar. He excused himself and left us alone. The old friend was Brandi, our dentist's wife. Now to me, that was plain stupid, but I was feeling too mellow to think on it long. Plus, Sugar was looking too good to think about anything else but her.

"So tell me about this feeling stuff," I said with as much bass, sincerity, and romance in my voice as possible.

"Look at you trying to be Mr. Suave. Where is this coming from?" Damn, this girl was feelin' me. I could only laugh.

"What are you talking about?"

"I'm talking about the mack-daddy routine. You sitting there licking your lips and looking all deep into my eyes. You got your leg all up against mine, you ain't looked at none of the other women in here, and you running your finger all up and down my arm. Did you forget Martha said ain't gon be none of that in her house tonight? So why you trying to get me all worked up? I ain't had a man the way I wanted in a long time. I am not the one to play with."

"Martha ain't got the only house in the city," I said.

"What are you saying?"

"I'm saying, Ricky's a big boy, he can get himself home." The words weren't out my mouth good before she was up and headed for the door. I gave Ricky the sign and followed right behind her.

The drive back to my home went so fast that I really don't remember it. Sugar asked me if I thought Ricky would ever really settle down and I said as far as I knew he had. She gave me a "yeah right" look and let it go.

Ricky was the type of man who I thought would always have other women. He was married to a woman who never really tried to catch him in his infidelity, and he cheated with women who didn't really want him. There was no love involved in his affairs. I doubt that there was even much sexual lust.

It was all in the conquest for men like him. He enjoyed romancing new women and he romanced them well. He lied and said he didn't, but I'd been told he bought his women diamonds and furs. Women got the attention of a new suitor, and Ricky got a new conquest. Ricky said the attraction was in his smile and processed hair. I said it was in his wallet.

When Sugar and I got to my bedroom I wanted to undress her, but she said no, and that she would meet me in the shower. I stood in that shower for twenty minutes waiting. I figured she might have changed her mind. Perhaps, seeing Brother Yazz put him back on her mind. After all, he'd been basically raping her for months. That wasn't something a person got over easily. Maybe I was rushing her. When I stepped from the shower into my bedroom, I expected to see her sitting on the bed crying. What I saw was my empty .22 ankle holster.

Four

High on my list of least favorite things is police in my house. Higher on my list of least favorite things is police in my house questioning me about a murder.

Yes, I was involved in a confrontation with Brother Yazz at All Star Liquors. Yes, I owned a '96 pearl white Fleetwood. Yes, my firearms were registered. No, I was not certain if shots were fired during the confrontation. No, I had no idea that Brother Yazz was found dead in his church. No, I had no plans on leaving town. No, my car was not available. I lent it to a friend. No, I didn't know if my friend had any known associations with Brother Yazz. Yes, I knew Richard Brown. Yes, we were together earlier. Yes, the confrontation was more between Mr. Brown and Brother Yazz. No, I was not a member of The New Day Brothers. No, I had no idea if Mr. Brown and Brother Yazz had confrontations in the past. Yes, of course I would call with any information I felt was relevant. Yes, I owned a .22 caliber pistol. No, it was not available. I kept it in the glove compartment of the car that was on loan. The car was on loan to Ms. Sugar Greer.

No, I did not know her current whereabouts. Of course I would have her call as soon as she returned the car. Yes, I arrived home before eleven PM.

It was three AM, and Ricky had not returned any of my 911 pages before the police detectives arrived, so I saw little purpose in paging him again. My restless mood was affecting the dogs. They paced the floor with me. The only plan I could come up with, after an hour or so of pacing and talking to the dogs, was to go out and look for Sugar. I decided to take the dogs with me.

My '73 Eldorado started on the first crank. I keep it in the backyard under a tarp. The light beams from the overhead streetlight in the alley had the black El-dog and the red vinyl top looking good in the darkness. I had a fresh coat of black paint put on a month ago. I was folding the tarp and about to place it in the trunk when my dogs began their warning growl. One was on each side of me, their ears were lowered, and their hind legs were cringed down. They were about to bolt.

I turned from the trunk and saw about four uniformed policemen approaching with guns drawn. I gave my dogs the command to heel. Yin did not comply. He was still in attack mode. I had to yank his collar to break his concentration. I gave the command to sit and they both sat. Yin's ears were still lowered and he was still baring his teeth. I shouted the command so the police would know the dogs were under control.

The officer leading the group was a brother, and he had his gun pointed directly at Yin. I told the dogs to lie down. They complied. The officer continued to advance, taking aim. He wanted to shoot my dog. I stood in front of Yin and yelled.

"These are trained dogs. They follow commands. There is no danger here." A white officer forced the brother to lower his gun. It was a good thing, because I would'a shot the brother before I let him shoot my dog.

"Mr. David Price, you are under arrest. Please lay face down on the ground with your arms extended." The white officer gave the order. I lay on the ground between my dogs and told the officers where my weapons were. My dogs did not budge while they yanked me from the ground, searched, and cuffed me. I had to keep my eyes on Yin. He wanted the black officer's ass.

When Fred, my next-door neighbor entered the yard, I gave the command "friend" and nodded in his direction. My dogs stood immediately and went behind him. Fred, who is scared shitless of my dogs, held his composure pretty well as they approached and stood behind him.

"What's the problem, officers?" Fred asked.

"This ain't your business, sir," the black officer snapped at him. "Please leave the yard."

What Fred said next earned him good Christmas gifts from me for the rest of my life.

"I live here. I got a right to know what's going on." Fred was saving my dogs from the pound. If a resident was home, and the animals posed no threat, the police had no right to impound them. I saw Fred's hand trembling as he patted Yang on the head.

"Mr. Price is being arrested as a suspect in the murder of Raymond Owens."

I knew it.

"Raymond Owens?" Fred asked.

"The Most Righteous Brother Yazz!" the black officer answered. I guessed that this brother was probably one of them New Day fools.

The four squad cars they sent to arrest me had my whole block lit up with blue flashing lights. It was kind of embarrassing, being hauled to jail in front of my neighbors. Although the police arresting folks was not something new in the neighborhood, it was new for them to be arresting me. I was just elected president of the newly formed block club, my first elected office.

Growing up in Chicago and spending a fair amount of time in the street, I'd been arrested before. I knew what to expect, but little about this arrest was expected. I wasn't printed, they didn't take me to the neighborhood lock up or the county. They took me straight to Twelfth Street and sat me down in an office. This was some new shit, and that concerned me.

Detectives Lee and Dixon, the same ones who came to my house earlier, entered the office. Looking at them, I couldn't help but notice what a strange pair they were. Dixon was a dark-skinned brother with very bad skin and no taste in clothes. Lee was a high yellow brother with red dreadlocks. He dressed like a star and appeared to keep a smile on his face.

Lee started it off, talking to my back. Neither of them sat at the desk with me.

"First off, that shit you told us earlier wasn't cute at all. You were the one shooting the guns at the liquor store. Your car, which was on loan to *Mrs. Sugar Owens,* was found down the block from the New Day Brothers church. And the .22 caliber we found next to the deceased is yours. So guess what, smart ass?"

"It sounds like I need a lawyer."

"Oh yeah, you right about that." It was Dixon's turn. "You fucked with us for no reason. You knew Sugar Greer was married to Brother Yazz. Is that why you killed him? You snuck in the church and popped him over a piece of pussy? Usually it's the preacher fucking somebody's wife. You decided to switch the shit up, huh? Fuckin' the preacher's wife, and then killing the preacher. Ain't that some shit?"

I was getting pissed, but not for the reasons he thought.

Hearing him talk about preachers fucking wives was closer to home than he really wanted to be. He saw my fist clench so he pushed a little further.

"Was she worth it? How was that holy pussy? Did God bless the preacher with a good piece of ass? Does she give good head? Did y'all pray first?"

The truth of what he said suddenly hit me. I was switching the tables. I was about to fuck a preacher's wife, not the same preacher who was with my wife, but a preacher nonetheless. I started laughing.

"What's so funny?" Dixon asked in my face. Three distinct odors assaulted my nose—stale coffee, cigarettes, and fried cabbage. I turned my head.

"Man, I didn't kill that nigga." I couldn't stop laughing. A habit I've had since childhood was laughing out loud at jokes in my mind. "And I think y'all know that. I ain't answering no questions without," I kept laughing, "my lawyer. If I am fucking a preacher's wife, that ain't no crime as far as I know."

"Discharging a firearm within city limits is a crime," Dixon said.

"I was protecting my client at the time, Mr. Richard Brown." My laughter subsided.

"And where is Mr. Brown?"

"Probably at home." I stood and put my cuffed hands in smiling Lee's face. I gave him a smile of my own.

"Where is Mrs. Sugar Owens?" Lee asked.

"I couldn't tell you." I jingled my cuffs, still smiling.

"She was identified at the church."

"I told you, I don't know where she is."

They didn't want me unless I gave them a confession. They were reaching. Sugar was their prime suspect. I was a second thought.

"Let him go. We can always find his giggling ass," Dixon said.

That tickled me more. I laughed all the way out the front door. I was still laughing when I got to the corner. I stopped when I realized the police had my Fleetwood. God only knew when I would get it back.

I walked up the block to Roosevelt Street and debated about catching the L train or a cab. When a silver Mercedes limo pulled up in front of me, blocking my path, I resisted the impulse to draw my pistols and watched the rear window lower.

I have seen men with grief stricken faces, men in agony over the loss of a loved one, but none matched the face that was behind the lowered black glass. This man had lost someone he loved a lot.

"Mr. Price, my name is Brother Jamal. Mother Owens would like to meet with you, if that's possible?" His eyes were pleading. I got into the limo for three reasons. First, I sensed no danger from Brother Jamal. Second, I needed information. At this point, I only had the information Sugar gave me on the New Day Brothers and Brother Yazz. True, the police allowed me to leave. But I knew it would only be a matter of time before they would seek me again, especially if neither of us found Sugar. Someone had to be blamed for Brother Yazz's murder, and they had all but told me I was next in line. Third, I needed a ride, and I had never ridden in a Mercedes limo.

Sugar said she turned to Brother Jamal for comfort. I could see why. He appeared to be a compassionate fellow. Dressed in his off-white linens, he kept a tissue at his nose and eyes. The man was weeping. Physically, he put me in the mind of Brother Yazz—same skin tone, similar hair and stature.

"I know you are aware that we lost Brother Yazz this evening."

"Yes. I was questioned regarding his death."

"Well, we have no control over who the police question. Mother Owens gave them a detailed description of the woman she saw leaving the church."

I found it odd that he referred to Sugar as "the woman," but I didn't comment. I didn't know how much they knew about my involvement. The fact that Brother Yazz's mama wanted to see me told me they knew something.

"What does she want to talk to me about?"

"I'm not certain, Mr. Price. I only know she wants to see you. Excuse me, please." His weeping intensified. I decided not to push. I was going to sit back and enjoy the ride in the limo until Brother Jamal placed a stack of photographs in my lap. "I'm sure it has something to do with these."

The photos dated back three weeks. The older ones were of Sugar and Ricky together. They were mostly taken at night. One was of them entering McDonald's on Eighty-third and Ashland, another was of them entering the library on Ninety-fifth and Halsted, and two had them entering the motel on Ninety-fifth and Racine. The last one was the only one taken during the day. They were entering City Hall. The pictures of Sugar and me were taken at IHOP, driving to Ricky's house, and leaving The Other Place. Brother Jamal didn't say a word as I studied the photos. I could tell he was waiting for a response. I gave him none. I stacked the photos and handed them back to him.

"I am not sure if you knew Sister Owens was married to The Most Righteous, but you can see by those photos that she wasn't worthy."

"Huh?"

"She was cheating on him! He gave her a new life and she went back to the world!" His eyes again filled with tears.

"Brother Jamal, those photos simply show her meeting with people."

"I know the type of meetings that take place at motels, Mr. Price. I was not always in the fold." Indignation is what took the place of grief in his eyes. I chose to look away. My own thoughts were breaking open like dropped eggs.

Ricky had pulled me into some of his mess. Sugar was more than what she seemed. Martha was right. Ricky and Sugar were more alike than I imagined. They were putting the moves on Brother Yazz, and something went wrong, or did it? What was supposed to be my part—keep Sugar safe while Ricky brought Brother Yazz down? Was there information that could bring the organization down? Was Brother Yazz looking for Sugar? Who was in danger? Brother Yazz, Sugar, me, Ricky?

The library and City Hall I understood—gathering information on properties, I guessed. But the motel, now that one had me. Martha said Ricky had been sending Sugar money for quite a while. Was Ricky capable of fucking Martha's sister? Did Martha suspect it? What was it she said? "She shared everything with her, but it wasn't enough."

I stopped myself. I was reaching. The motel photos had me tripping. People did meet at motels, especially when they were meeting in secret. That's what I settled my mind with as I continued my first Mercedes limo ride.

Four guard dogs patrolled Mother Owens' home. Two were red female Dobermans, and the others were gray German shepherds. Shepherds are smart dogs, but my preference is Dobermans. People seldom try Dobermans because they are respected and feared. The two female Dobermans looked as if they might breed well with my boys. Later, if this all worked out well, I'd bring them over for a date. The next thing I knew, my thoughts were on how well Sugar and I would breed. I pictured us at Ricky's on a Saturday with our own set of twin girls. I could almost smell the caramel cake when the limo door was opened.

"This way please, Mr. Price."

Mother Owens had bought herself one of those Frank Lloyd Wright homes in Beverly. Chicago's Beverly Hills had always been a prestigious place to reside. Homes sat on large hills. The only thing keeping them from being estates was that they were located on city blocks. Over the past fifteen years, blacks in the city had gained enough wealth to purchase in the area. To my surprise, Mother Owens's living room was identical in furnishing and interior design to Ricky's. Sugar's touch was apparent. An obvious exception was a life-sized bronze statue. At first glance, I thought it was Brother Yazz, but the statue was shorter, and the man it was modeled after was older. The first line of the inscription at the base read, "He will always be with us." The second line stated, "The Elder Pastor Owens." Brother Jamal offered me the high back chair next to a Tiffany lamp.

"Have a seat. Mother Owens will be with you shortly." He left without a goodbye. He was still miffed because I told him people met in motels. Sitting in the room, admiring the surroundings, Sugar crept back into my mind and it was a purely carnal thought. I wanted to find her, and once I found her, I had every intention of fucking her brains out. She owed me a good fuck, and I was ready to collect.

If she and Ricky kicked it, so what? If she killed Brother Yazz, so what? I was arrested, my Fleetwood was impounded, and her panties hung in my bathroom. She slept in my bed. She drank my Remy, cooked me dinner, and sang me to sleep. I had to have her, and I had to find her before the police did. I wasn't up to waiting twenty years to get some ass. I attributed the lilacs I smelled to remembering Sugar, but I was wrong.

"Mr. Price?"

I stood merely because her presence required it. The woman was regal. It was five in the morning, and she was dressed for a state dinner, complete with pearls, silk stockings, and a royal blue evening gown with one of those high, hidden splits. Her hair was pulled up into a crown that fell back into a thick braid which hung halfway down her back. The royal blue softened those cold, steel-gray eyes. *No stupid*, I told myself. *It was the death of her son that softened her eyes*. Brother Yazz was, I guessed, ten years my junior, and his mother couldn't have been ten years my senior. If she was, God had certainly blessed her.

"Yes, Mrs. Owens, and I'm sorry for your loss."

"Thank you. Have a seat, please. I won't take up much of your time." I returned to my seat in the high back chair.

"No, please join me here on the sofa. I doubt the ability of my voice to carry across this room." I sat with two sofa cushions separating us, but her scent was as strong as Sugar's in my Fleetwood.

"Mr. Price . . ."

"David, please." I don't know why I told the woman to call me David.

"David, I know you are aware that my son was killed tonight." She held her hand up to stop me from interrupting. She had manicured nails, diamonds on each finger except the index, and her wrist was encircled with diamond tennis bracelets. Either Sugar imitated her, or she imitated Sugar.

"I told the police that I saw Sugar running from the church. I didn't intend to implicate her in his death. She wouldn't kill him. Hurt him, maybe, but killing is not in her nature. I know she's spent the last day or so in your company." She looked at me as if I should have been surprised, but I kept a straight face to let her know I wasn't. She was a woman with money. Information was one of her privileges. "I hired a detective. Sugar was not happy here her last days, for reasons I'd rather not discuss. Prison altered my son."

She was the second fine woman I had watched cry in twenty-four hours. I pulled two Kleenex from the holder under the lamp and handed them to her.

"Thank you, David. I hired the detective to find out about Sugar's past. I knew about her recent past, the drug addiction and prostitution. But I wanted to know where she came from. The detective insisted on following her. When he showed me the first photographs, I was honestly shocked. I told Raymond to let her go. It was obvious she wanted her old life back. But he felt it was only a phase, a temporary backslide. He was going to confront her with the pictures, but she ran away.

"Then the detective brought pictures of you. Raymond seemed unaffected. He said she had a lot on her mind. If he loved her, I didn't see it. She was a possession, like all the Mercedes, all the liquor stores, and even this house. He bought one across the street for himself, although this house was big enough for all of us. But the Raymond prison produced, Brother Yazz, wanted to live apart from his mother. He, Jamal, and Sugar shared that house.

"If you know where Sugar is, David, please tell her to come home. We have more to discuss than she knows. I have hired lawyers for her defense. Tell her that the child she carries will not be born in prison."

"Child?"

"She didn't tell you? She's pregnant with Raymond's child. I have instructed Paul Phillips, he is the detective in my employ, to assist you in finding her if you do not know of her whereabouts. Because he is Caucasian, he may not be privy to some of the places she might return to. Here is his card, and of course I will pay all your fees and expenses. If you can get her to call me, that will be enough."

"This is not the type of work I . . ."

"Please, David." She stopped my refusal. "I need your help. If she turns back to drugs, you and I both know the effect that will have on the baby. That child must be born healthy. That child is more important than her or me. It is the continuation of my husband. He must be born healthy."

She stopped talking and I couldn't think of anything to say. The news of Sugar being pregnant made me gag.

"If you will excuse me, I have a photo shoot scheduled in a few moments. Life must go on. My driver will take you to your destination. Goodbye and I hope to hear from you shortly."

I tried to pump the limo driver for information about Brother Yazz, Jamal, and Sugar's living arrangements, but he rolled the glass barrier up on me. After meeting Brother Jamal, the scene seemed kind of freaky to me. Why would a man have another man living with him and his wife? Brother Jamal did not strike me as the bodyguard type, maybe a personal valet. The strange living arrangement and the news about Sugar being pregnant curbed my carnal thoughts about her.

When I entered my house, my mutts didn't greet me at the front door, which was unusual. I figured Fred kept them at his house. I headed straight to the refrigerator, but stopped at the kitchen table. I noticed a white, leather, attaché case with my keys lying on top of it. Sugar had taken my keys when she took my Fleetwood. I drew my pistols and crept up the stairs. I heard her humming, and damn it, she sounded sweet. I holstered my guns and entered my bedroom.

My mutts were stretched out on the floor at the foot of my bed. Sugar was stretched out on my bed, naked as a peach. I gave Yin and Yang the command to guard and closed the door on them. As I said before, I am not a stranger to beautiful women. Sugar's big, full breasts, flat stomach, thin waist, thick thighs, and pelvic hair as curly as the hair on her head did not stop me from asking questions. Neither did the skin that looked as soft as Minnie Ripperton's voice. What stopped me was the slow, twisting tongue she slid along my clenched lips. I wanted to ask questions, but at that moment, they seemed unimportant. Once again her ebony eyes encased in ivory captured my thoughts.

I hadn't heard the tune "Just a Memory" in years, but as Sugar pulled me to the bed, it was just as clear in my mind as if Duke and J. Hodges were in the room. The music filled my head as I filled Sugar's body.

I woke up later that morning alone. What we did in that bed went beyond fucking. The physical, being too intense to stay in the physical, goes into the emotional and thus, one makes love or at least a strong infatuation. Before Sugar fell asleep in my arms, she whispered, "This dick is mine." It made me smile. I expected to wake with my chin in her curls, but being alone didn't alarm me. Her black dress hung from the back of the bedroom door. The bathroom door opened and she walked into the bedroom.

She smiled when she noticed I was awake. I found myself staring at her stomach as she walked toward me. If Brother Yazz's seed was in there, it wasn't showing. She didn't slide next to me as I had hoped. Instead, she propped up two pillows and sat facing me with her knees up and her thighs opened wide. I no longer stared at her stomach. She was offering me breakfast, and I didn't hesitate.

As a younger man, my head wouldn't have been nestled between her thighs. As the man I am now, I enjoy the opportunity to show off my experience. It impressed some women, and I was back to trying to impress her. When I felt her hands settle on the back of my head, I knew she was getting impressed. When she gripped my head and held it in place, I knew it wouldn't be long. When her thighs clamped around my ears and she dug her nails into my shoulders and screamed, "Sweet Jesus!" and released enough juice to drink, I knew she was impressed.

When I looked up, the ebony stones were rolled back in her head and I could only see ivory. Normally, I would have stopped at that point and allowed her to gather herself, but my jones was so hard that the skin was binding. I slid straight into her.

If it was English she was speaking, I didn't recognize it. It sounded like she was talking in tongues. I held my weight off her until I felt my own orgasm arriving. I put my hands beneath her, gripping her butt as tight as I could and allowing all two hundred and thirty pounds to grind into her pelvis. All I could say was, "Sugar."

The red numbers on the clock on my dresser read 2:30. Sugar was asleep on my chest. I kissed her forehead and eased out of bed to go to the bathroom. I can't lie, I was weak at the knees and I had to steady myself against the shower wall. The last person I pushed myself to that level of performance for was my ex-wife.

We had been separated for about two months, and Martha invited us both over to dinner, neither of us knowing the other was coming. I was living temporarily in a small studio apartment in Harvey. We said we were going to talk, but as soon as we entered the apartment, we started stripping. She'd gained a little weight and was thicker in the hips. Being a thin woman, every pound was noticed, but the additional weight excited me, something new on something familiar. Her hips had spread once before when she was pregnant with Eric. But our wanting didn't allow me to spend a second thought on anything but her.

In my mind, she left me because the preacher had done a better job in the bed than I had. I didn't want her back, but I wanted her to feel what she was giving up. That was the last time I can remember experiencing four orgasms in this decade.

Two on a good night, three on a great night, but seldom four. Four orgasms meant sore stomach muscles, weak knees, tight back, sore jones, stiff neck, extra vitamins, an egg protein drink, and at least ten hours of sleep. It wasn't like I couldn't do four on a regular basis. I simply didn't like paying the price for four.

I was too tired to bathe and shower, so I settled for just a shower. As the hot water ran from my head to my toes, I thought of my ex-wife. More than four years had passed since I last saw her. After our night at the apartment, we avoided each other. I didn't see her again until my grandmama's funeral months later. She'd gained a little weight and she was very distant.

I questioned why I would think of her with Sugar in my bed. I hadn't thought of her after having sex with other women, but for some reason I felt guilty. It didn't make any sense to feel guilty. I was a divorced man and had every right to be with a beautiful woman.

Regina said it was my fault that she and the preacher got together. She'd gone to him to talk about our marriage, Eric's death, and me. She begged me to go to the sessions with her, but I didn't believe another man had the answer to my marriage or to my son's death. I didn't think I would find it between another woman's thighs either, but that's where I went. I expected Regina to wait until I worked it out. She expected me to work it out with her. We grew apart, and the preacher moved into the space that was left.

The night I followed them downtown to the Hotel Nikko, I knew what to expect when I kicked the door in. However, I was unprepared for the pain of seeing his skinny, wrinkled up ass riding my wife from the back. I also wasn't prepared for her words when she looked back at me.

"Close the door, David. There is nothing here you want," she said through tears, and she was right. There was no reason to put a bullet in the preacher's head or hers. Our marriage was over. I went home and packed my things. Walking out the front door, my eye caught the gold leafed Bible my parents had given us on our wedding day. I stood there staring at that Bible for over an hour, waiting for—almost demanding some type of guidance. If it came, I didn't hear it. I left the Bible there for her. This was the life she wanted, and she could have it all, including the omnipotent God that allowed my son to die.

I switched the water in the shower from hot to cold, shivered, and put my mind back on Sugar. All my thoughts, as far as Sugar was concerned, were questions, questions that had to be answered for me to move ahead in my mind. I had a place for her, but I had to clear the way first. Brother Yazz was in the way, the police were in the way, Ricky was in the way. I told myself that whatever she told me, I was going to believe it.

Then I thought about an ostrich with its head in the sand and a hyena on its ass. I would hear what she had to say before I decided to believe her. To my surprise, when I stepped out the shower Sugar was sitting on the toilet peeing. Her forced familiarity was back in full force.

"I left you some hot water," I said and smiled in her direction while trying not to look at her sitting on the toilet.

"Why thank you, Mr. Man. That was awful generous of you." Then she farted. "I think you'd better leave unless you really want to get to know me!" she said, laughing and not at all embarrassed. My exit was quick. I did want to get to know her, but that part could wait.

I stretched out across my king-size bed and grabbed the remote from the nightstand. I flipped on the small Sony television on my dresser. *Harlem Nights* was on cable. It was the scene where Della Reese was kicking Eddie Murphy's butt in the alley. I loved this movie for a couple of reasons. First, was the casting of three generations of black comedians—Redd Foxx, Richard Pryor, and Eddie Murphy. Another reason was the point made in the film about family amongst hustlers. I was fluffing up a pillow, getting ready for a comfortable viewing when the phone rang. It was Ricky.

Yes, Sugar was okay. Yes, she was with me. Yes, the police took me in. No, I was not charged. Yes, they were assholes. Yes, I told them he was involved. Yes, those were my 911 pages. Yes, they had my Fleetwood, and, yes, that was a bitch. Yes, they wanted to question Sugar. Yes, I knew *Harlem Nights* was on cable. Yes, I would have Sugar call him when she was available. Yes, I knew she was a good person with some problems. No, we hadn't talked about him yet, but we were planning on it. No, we didn't need his input on what to do next. Yes, I knew his ass was on the line as well. No, I didn't know the police pulled him in for questioning. Yes, I knew they found my gun at the murder scene. Yes, I gave my gun to Sugar. No, I hadn't asked her about it. What have we been doing?

"Fuckin' like bunnies!" I said, and hung up the phone.

"Was that Ricky?" Sugar asked, walking toward the

bed, smelling surprisingly fresh, like a rose garden after a rain.

"Yeah, that was his tired ass." She slid next to me on my pillow. It didn't make any sense at all. I wasn't in any shape to be starting nothing, but I took her left breast into my mouth. It was a peach, a big, firm peach, and I couldn't resist. She pulled away.

"Oh no, not again. We got work to do."

That's what came out of her mouth, but what I saw in her eyes was, "If you really want to, go ahead." So I did. As soft, shriveled up, and wore out as he was, my jones had the nerve to try to get hard. Neither my stomach muscles, back, nor knees were having it. They sent a message straight to my brain—"Stop that fool before he kills us!" Sugar's message, however, was a bit stronger.

"Oooh, David, is that what I think it is beating against my thigh? I know you can't be serious. How old did you say you are? Look at him trying to stretch out. You mind if I help?"

What that woman did next, I do believe spoiled me for life. Never has a woman put her mouth on me in that fashion. I say mouth because she used every part of it—jaws, tongue, teeth, lips, and her throat. The red numbers read 3:15 when she started. It was 4:45 when I yanked the straps free from my box spring and let go of number five.

She started out so gentle, hardly disturbing me while I watched *Harlem Nights*—a little lick here, a little kiss there, and a little suck underneath. I lay back on the pillow and relaxed, certain it wasn't going to get much more intense. She was merely cooing, pecking here and there. When she switched gears, I remained cool.

The sucking increased, but it was still very gentle and the kisses became short sucks that popped. The licks were longer. They went from tip to base. I stayed in control and gave an encouraging, "Go on girl with your bad self!" The scene with Della Reese fussing with Red Foxx about having her mouth fixed and ready for hash was on.

It was when Sugar's sucks started getting as long as the licks that I knew I was in trouble. I switched off the Sony. She was sucking from tip to base. Half of my jones was in her mouth, and her tongue continued to twist around it. I tried to pull out. I didn't want to cum in her mouth, but she wrapped her arms around my waist and locked her lips. When I felt her swallowing my jones, bit by bit, I stopped trying to retreat and let her go at it. Baby girl obviously knew what she was doing. She must have felt my jones loading up to shoot, because she backed up off him.

She put her mouth around my balls and started humming. I was on edge from both pleasure and fear. The vibrations from her humming had my toes spread, but the fear from her teeth on the top of my ball sack had my fists clenched. A brother was on overload. I didn't know whether to scream or moan. When I felt her teeth open, I sighed and moaned, thinking she was going to leave my balls alone, but she didn't. She went at them with her tongue and lips. She separated them with her tongue and cupped them with her lips, she meshed them together almost to the point of pain, then released them into the warmth and softness of her saliva filled mouth. I begged her to stop. She covered my mouth with her hand and climbed on top of me.

I had been ridden well before, but no one rode me like Sugar. Once she was on top of me, my jones was hers. I had no control over what she did to it or where it went once it was inside of her. She yanked it to and fro, and stretched it with circular gyrations. I was certain she would pull it from my body. When she rose up, she pulled it with her. When she slammed down, she took it deep inside her. When she arched her back up, she curved it inside. She pulled it as long as she wanted and held it as tight as she wanted. She popped it at the joint, and damn it hurt, but not enough to push her off. I snatched the straps from the box spring and said some shit in a language far from English.

When she rolled off of me, I swear I didn't recognize my own jones. The motherfucker was longer than I'd ever seen it. I think she said something like, "You mine now," but I ain't sure, 'cause number five put me out.

When I woke up, Sugar was dressed and sitting at the foot of the bed. As a man who'd done his best lovemaking of the decade, I was a bit annoyed by the fact that she was up and dressed. As far as I was concerned, she too, should have been curled up in a fetal position, dreaming of butterflies in a field sucking on peach blossoms.

"I ran you a bath, David. We've got to get started." She stood and walked to the bathroom door. "Come on, up and at it!" she said and clapped her hands rapidly the way Mrs. Sargent, my old Sunday school teacher did when the boys weren't paying attention. I quickly sat erect, just like I did in Sunday school.

Almost alert, I looked again to Sugar's stomach. I beckoned her to me.

"Oh no, I ain't getting close to you. I know your moves." She was smiling, but she was ready to go.

"I just need to ask you something."

"Ask me from here," she said, standing in front of the bathroom door.

"Are you pregnant with Brother Yazz's child?" Direct was the only way I talked to people I cared about.

"Why?"

"I need to know."

"Why?"

" 'Cause."

" 'Cause ain't a reason."

"Are you?"

"No, and if I was, what difference would it make?"

"What?"

"What difference would it make if I was pregnant with another man's child? How would that affect you protecting me?"

"It wouldn't affect my protecting you, but it would affect our relationship."

"Our relationship, David, is you protecting me."

"What?"

She walked to the bed and sat down next to me. "Don't do this. Don't make something more of what we did here, please. We have a business relationship, one I need now more than ever before."

I didn't want her eyes to match what was coming from her mouth, but they did. I saw no emotion, no caring, nothing. Her face was all about business. I must've heard her wrong. My dick wasn't hers. She reminded me of the first prostitute I'd slept with. I told her I loved her, she told me she loved my money. As I did with the prostitute, I ran from her presence. I wrapped myself in the top sheet, stood, and walked past her to the bathroom.

I didn't bathe in the water she drew. Instead, I took a hot-ass shower. I told myself that what I felt for Sugar went down the drain with the suds. When I came out of the bathroom with a towel wrapped around my waist, she was still sitting on the bed.

"Excuse me while I get dressed. I'll meet you downstairs."

Our eyes met for a second and I thought I saw something more, but she looked down and said, "Fine." She left, pulling the door behind her. I restrained myself from yelling "bitch" at her back. I dressed quickly because if I slowed down, I might have stopped. I might have sat down and felt the hurt that was trying to come. I was good at moving too fast for hurt to catch me. If nothing else, I knew how to outrun it.

My Cobra 9 mm felt good in my hands. My customized holster felt even better when I strapped it on. I was on the job. I was moving. I ripped the sheets from the bed and stuffed them into my laundry bag. "It wasn't nothing but some good ass," I told myself as I slammed the closet door shut. The large framed picture of my grandmama holding Eric fell from the wall when the closet door slammed. I had to slow down to pick it up. The glass wasn't broken. I sat on the bed and looked at them both. They both left too soon. What was it Martha said? *Slow down and feel the pain.* No. I kissed the picture and laid it across my bare mattress. Not today.

Sugar was pulling the dogs' dry food from the pantry when I entered the kitchen.

"Don't feed my damn dogs!" It came out as nasty as I intended. She immediately withdrew her hands from the bag. "Yin, Yang outside!" They hesitated, but followed my command. I snatched open the refrigerator door, took out the food she'd cooked earlier, and filled their bowls with it. I didn't look in her direction as I carried it outside to them.

When I came back into the kitchen, she was running dishwater for the pots and bowls. I stopped her.

"Look, this is my home, those are my dogs, and those are my dishes. As a client, none of them require a damn thing from you. What you need to do is sit your ass down and tell me about last night. Tell me why my gun was found at a murder scene. Tell me why Brother Yazz's mama saw your ass running from the church. Tell me why you snuck out of here last night. Tell me why the fuck you left my ride for the police to take. That's the shit you should be concerned with. Them damn dishes ain't your concern!"

"Why you talking to me like that?" she asked, sitting at the table. "What have I done?"

"You ain't done shit to me yet, and I ain't gonna let cha! The motherfuckin' police came into my home, took me downtown, and questioned me like I was a fuckin' murderer. This is you and Ricky's shit, I see that now, but since I'm in it, gotdamnit, I'ma know everything. Start with last night!" I sat across from her looking through her eyes. They were no longer ebony stones encased in ivory. I saw the rotten center of two peeled white potatoes.

"Maybe working together is not going to work out."

"It ain't your choice no more. I'm in it! Last night?"

"I don't have to take this!" she said, standing.

"You can take it from me or you can take it from the police. It would be a hellava lot easier for me to turn your ass over to them and I would be finished with this shit."

"You wouldn't." She returned to her seat.

"Baby girl, I sho would, in a motherfuckin' heartbeat. Talk to me, or talk to them." I wasn't playing.

"I didn't kill him. He was alive when I left. He and Jamal were in the office talking."

"Why did you go there?"

"To get my case. I figured with him out in the streets, it would be safe."

"Why didn't you tell me?"

"Because I wasn't coming back. Despite what you think, I didn't want to involve you or get you hurt."

"But you left my car and my gun?"

"It got crazy, David. I got in easy enough. But when I came out of the prayer room with my case, I saw his mother, so I ducked back in. She went back into the office. I thought it was my chance to sneak out, but she came out of the office screaming about his filthy sinning and how the wrath of the Lord would be upon him. I was a step away from the front door when she called my name. I couldn't hold the case and the gun, and open the door! I dropped the gun and ran. When I got back to the car, I couldn't work the keys, and she was running down the block after me with her two guards! When I got to the corner of Racine, a cab was sitting at the light. I jumped in, and he took me to the Greyhound station."

"What's in the case?"

"Money, jewels, and the ledgers."

"Why did you come back here?"

"What?"

"Why did you come back here?"

"I don't know. I mainly went back to the church for the money and the jewels. Once I got them, all I could think about was leaving. I was standing in line about to board the bus for Dallas, which was the first one out. But I saw this girl, Laverne. She was passing out New Day Brothers' literature. I used to get high with her. She didn't recognize me when she handed me one of his flyers. She told me God was the way and Brother Yazz spoke his message. Hearing her dedication, and seeing the belief in her eyes pulled me out of that line and back here. I got work to do, David."

"Brother Yazz is dead, in case you forgot."

"But the organization ain't. What I got in that case will kill it."

"Why didn't you just mail it to a newspaper?"

"Ricky said your ex-wife is a newspaper reporter."

"So."

"She can report the story."

"Oh shit, now I got it. You want me to convince her to do the story. Y'all sure went the long way around the block. Regina would have accepted the story on its merits, not on my recommendation."

"Ricky said it would be better if you took it to her."

"How long you and Ricky been working on this?"

"What?"

"How long have you and Ricky been putting this together?"

"A little while."

"How long?"

"Two years!"

"Two motherfucking years!" I jumped up from the table. I had to or else I would'a slapped her face. I'd been played and played well. I went to the living room and opened my bar. It was Grand-Dad time. I went back to the kitchen, sat at the table, yanked out the spout, and turned up the gallon.

"It's not like you think, David. When Ricky and your brother found me . . ."

"Wait . . . my brother, Robert?"

"Yeah, Ricky hired him to find me."

"Damn! Is everybody playing me?" She didn't answer my question.

"When they found me, I was cracked out. That part was true. I didn't want to get clean. I sure as hell didn't want to see Ricky or Martha. They tried so hard to help me. But your brother told me Ricky had a plan that would get me enough money to stay high for years. David, I was living like shit, worse than your brother. All Ricky wanted me to do was to go to the shelter and find out anything I could on Brother Yazz. It wasn't supposed to be a long, drawn-out process. Ricky was certain it wouldn't take me longer than a couple of weeks. He thought Brother Yazz was fucking his female followers. He was wrong.

"What happened was something Ricky didn't plan. I liked being clean. I began to believe in the new life

Brother Yazz promised. Weeks passed and I hadn't called Ricky, so he sent your brother to one of the services. I told him point blank, Brother Yazz was my savior and not to come around me anymore. He believed me and I think he was genuinely happy for me. He told me not to worry about Ricky. He would handle him. He's a lot like you, likes protecting people, especially women. Please stop drinking, David. I don't want you to get drunk."

"What!" I dared her with my eyes to say it again.

"Never mind. Anyway, after things changed between me and Brother Yazz, I found out about the books and some other shit and I called Ricky. We started meeting and put the plan together. We didn't set out to hurt you. You only became part of the plan when Ricky thought about taking the ledgers to the press. He said he asked you to help him, but you turned him down. He said you would help a woman in need faster than you would help him, so he introduced us. You were supposed to think about taking the information to your ex-wife. That was Ricky's plan.

"A damsel in distress was my part. It was an easy part to play. I was scared, but I didn't plan on using you. I didn't plan on liking your dogs or cooking you dinner. I didn't plan on seeing Laverne. I didn't know Robert was your brother. I've never been a damsel in distress, and I forgot how good it felt to be protected. I forgot how good it felt to be cared for, to be held, and to be called beautiful. I forgot how good it felt to be tucked in, to have a man please me because it pleased him, and to please a man because I wanted to please him, not because he had a cocaine rock, a warm place to stay, or a diamond tiara, but because I wanted to. I don't know why I came back here, David. I ain't never been a damsel in distress, only a bitch in need."

At that moment, her eyes didn't match the words she

had said earlier. At that moment, I saw the softness that was in my bed. I saw confusion, caring, and concern. I put the bottle down, picked up her hand, and kissed it.

"You were born a damsel, never a bitch."

She'd done it again, changed directions in midstream. Upstairs in my bedroom she told me we were nothing but business associates. Her tear-filled eyes now told me we were more than either of us could explain. It wasn't her fault; her eyes were saying that she acted like a bitch because she was a neophyte in dealing with the physical that moved into the emotional.

Five

Our plan was simple enough—call Ricky and Regina and set up a meeting at Regina's office. What bothered me was Sugar's certainty that the police would believe her story. She felt that if the Greyhound ticket was proof enough for me, it would also convince the police. I knew different.

Sugar was their prime suspect. It would take more than a ticket purchase to persuade them otherwise. I hoped the clerk on duty would remember her, or even the girl she'd gotten high with in the past. A witness to her whereabouts might convince them. My thought was to locate that witness before Sugar went to talk to the police. Hopefully Greyhound worked a three to eleven shift and the same clerk would be on duty.

Sugar wanted to go to Regina's office first. She wanted the ledgers out of her hands and into the hands of the media. I understood her urgency. My hesitancy was largely due to the fact that I hadn't spoken to Regina in over four years. Calling her was a little more difficult for me than simply dialing a phone number. How does one greet an ex-wife he hadn't spoken to in over four years? How does one casually say hello to the mother of his dead son? How does a man nonchalantly start a conversation with a woman who still managed to make him feel guilty four years after a divorce? I picked up the phone and dialed.

Regina answered the phone on the first ring.

"Regina Price." Her voice was crisp and polished. I knew she'd kept my name, but hearing her say it made me smile. I stuttered before I answered because I had to stop my old "Hey, baby."

"Hey, Gina, it's David."

"Hello, David?" Her voice was questioning. I didn't want to delay why I was calling.

"Gina, I got something going here, and you might be interested in doing a story on it." Sugar was listening and watching me intently. I didn't want to drop my eyes, so I looked into her face and talked to Regina. "It's about the New Day Brothers and Brother Yazz."

"The preacher that was just murdered?"

"One and the same."

"This must be the day for him. I got a call five minutes ago from a woman saying she had information linking Brother Yazz to the jewelry store robberies."

"No shit?" I looked down at Sugar's jeweled wrist and thought about the case.

"I speak the truth."

"Do you mind if I stop by in an hour or so?"

"No problem. It's going to be a late night for me anyway."

"Ricky and the source will be with me."

"Fine. It would be nice to see Ricky again. How deeply is he involved?"

"Deep."

"Is the source close to Brother Yazz?"

"His wife."

"Good! I look forward to meeting her. See you in an hour or so. Goodbye, David."

"Bye, Gina." It wasn't as hard as I had thought. After I hung up, I realized she said it would be good to see Ricky again and she was looking forward to meeting the source, but she said nothing about seeing me. I didn't harp on it. The jewelry store information pushed it out of my mind.

"Sugar, Regina said she got a call linking Brother Yazz to the jewelry store robberies. You know anything about that?" I didn't bother to look her in eyes when I asked. It was clear to me I couldn't read her lies. I dialed Ricky's number.

"I don't know. All I took were the jewels he gave me." I didn't ask her again. The truth would come out one way or another. It always did.

The call to Ricky went almost as smoothly as Regina's call. He wanted us to come to his house first and go over exactly what information Sugar was going to give to Regina. I told him we were no longer following his plan. The plan we had stood as it was. If he wanted to meet us at Regina's office, fine. If he didn't, fine. I would call him back and tell him what time to meet us there. The sharpness in my tone, along with hanging up while he was in mid-sentence let him know his original plan was no longer a secret. I was halfway expecting him to call back, but he didn't. I knew he was trying to figure out a way to cover his ass when he saw me. If he had an explanation for his deception, he would have called back. He didn't, so he was trying to formulate one.

Sugar sat across from me at the kitchen table snickering about me hanging up on Ricky. I laughed with her for a couple of seconds until the police entered my mind. Along with the ledgers, Sugar's attaché case held money and jewels, motive to the police. My thoughts were serious, and it must have shown on my face. But I didn't want to shake Sugar's confidence in the police believing her alibi. When she asked if everything was all right, I told her yes. I hid behind her original urgency and rushed her from the house.

Once in the backyard, she didn't let me rush her to the car. She stopped and babied my mutts. I stood in the middle of my backyard leaning against my Eldorado waiting for Sugar to finish petting and fussing over the dogs. While waiting, Englewood filled my senses. Nothing I heard, smelled, or saw was foreign to me. I was at home. From the faintest childlike whimper of a kitten trapped in a garage, to the distant bass line beat of Too Short, to the pigeon droppings that christened the hood of my freshly-painted Eldorado, to the acrobatic squirrel that sped along the high power lines, to the smell of overripe mulberries, to pungent, hot tar fumes from a rattling kettle being pulled behind an old truck covered with just as much tar as paint—for me, they all joined together to form my symphony of home—Englewood.

While driving, my mind was wandering, and that was a bad thing. The situation required my undivided attention. However, the thought of sitting in Regina's office with Sugar present made me uncomfortable. I could see Regina quickly evaluating the situation and coming to the conclusion that I was still whorish. Not that I was concerned about what she thought. I just didn't want her in my business, especially my romantic affairs.

Our marriage, for the most part, consisted of me trying to live up to her expectations of a man. I, or no other mortal male, would ever reach her expectations or her mother's. Her father died working three jobs trying to keep her mother happy. An uneducated brother who married a doctor's daughter, he was behind the eight ball from the beginning.

He died when Regina was a baby, and she formed her mythical man from the lies her mother told about her father. They had to be lies, because no man could ever do the things Regina's mother claimed her deceased husband did. The man worked three jobs, two full time and one part time. He maintained the lawn, kept the house painted, and helped her clean and cook. The man died at thirty-six, so maybe it was true. I don't know.

For Regina, a good man was faithful, strong, hardworking, church-going, and never drank or raised his voice in anger. All the money he earned, he gave to his wife and trusted her to do the right thing with it. His idea of a good time was church picnics, teas, and monthly revivals. Sex would be limited to every other Friday night (payday). He had no friends she didn't approve of, and he shared every thought in his head with her. She would buy all his clothes, and, of course, he drove the beat-up car while the new car was hers. On Sundays after church, he could watch one football game.

I tried to fit into the mold. I believed that becoming the man she wanted would benefit me. I knew when I married her what type of brother she was looking for. I acted like that type while we were dating. I told her I didn't drink, and I took her to my parents' church and introduced her to their preacher as if he was mine. I joined her church and even read the Bible with her. It wasn't all phony. I really believed I could have lived like that. I wanted to live like that. I was tired of hanging out on the streets and trying to make school work. I knew settling down was the best thing if I wanted to do something serious with my life.

Everything was cool until we had sex. The girl was a straight freak, and that shocked the shit out of me. She knew how to do things me and Ricky only talked about doing with women. At twenty-one I had been with a couple of women, but none of the round-the-way girls did half the shit she did. None of the good girls in Englewood sucked on you, and none of the fast ones ever asked me to stick it in their behinds.

I viewed her differently after we had sex. I started watching her, and I would catch her eyes on the slick niggas, the tailor-made-suit, processed-hair-wearing brothers, my niggas. The kind of brother I was before her. I didn't go back to being myself right away. I waited until after we were married. If she wanted to play the square girl, it was OK with me, as long as she stayed freaky in the bed.

A month or so after we were married I started taking her to nightclubs—The Copher Box, The GodFather, and The Club. I brought beer to our little place and started smoking a little weed. I thought she'd be cool with it. After a week, she packed up her stuff and moved back to Glencoe with her mother. To get her back I had to tell her I was only backsliding. I promised her Jesus was the center of my life, and drinking, smoking weed, and clubbing were behind me. She told me she'd given up her sinful life before she met me, and she understood how easy it was to backslide, but if I was to be her husband, I had to give up worldly things and truly seek God. She loved me, but she wasn't going to let me lead her back down hell's path. God spared her from a life of sin. She was no longer a foolish teenager who looked for sinful thrills. She was a married woman, and she was ready to act like one.

I lasted for about two years, then I started sneaking out with Ricky. I didn't go out with Ricky to chase women, although that was his main focus. Being out with him did put me in some compromising situations, but I remained faithful to Regina. I went out with Ricky because I was bored. The church did not fill me as it did Regina. I needed more than the belief that I was living to please God. I needed action. And going out with Ricky always got me into something: fights, car races, crap games, high sessions, anything was bound to happen. Sneaking out provided action. If Regina knew I was going out, she acted like she didn't.

I still went to church, but I stopped trying to be saved. Church became a place I went to make my wife happy. I lived like that for about seven years, going to church and pretending to be the man Regina wanted me to be. My life was OK. I had a career, a pretty wife, and my best friend and I could sneak out every now and then. I loved and needed my wife. If this was the kind of life she wanted, I was willing to live it for her. I loved Regina more than I loved anyone, until Eric was born.

He was born premature and with a weak heart. I prayed the whole week he was in the incubator. I promised God that if he let my son live, my life was his. The week he came home I went to church and told the preacher about my promise to God. He told me to increase my tithes and to walk in God's light. Everything I did from that point on had to be God-centered. I was to ask myself what would God want me to do before I did anything. "Seek him first," he told me. To be truthful, it made my life a lot easier.

When faced with the temptation of drinking, drugging, or gambling, I prayed and asked God to help me. I viewed myself as a lost sheep seeking God's help. When I was upset at work, I prayed and asked for God's guidance. I accepted whatever happened as God's will. It wasn't my wife trying to change me. It was me getting right with God.

For the first time in my life, the Bible started making

sense. I understood scripture. I looked forward to Tuesday night Bible study and Sunday school. I felt God's presence in everything I did—driving my car, walking down the street, rocking my son in my arms, and making love to my wife. God was with me always. I felt him the most in the morning when I woke. It was as if God personally woke me up every morning. I woke with prayer and praises for him. I was walking in his light. I was that lost sheep the preacher spoke about, the one that found his way home.

The first change I noticed in my life once I started putting God first was my own calmness. Hardly anything could raise my anger. Everything was OK because God was in control. When I was passed over for a promotion at the hospital, it was all right. It was God's will. When we were denied the loan for the house in a white suburb, it was all right. God would work it out. When someone broke into our little apartment on Eighty-seventh and Ashland and stole our new television, stereo, and all our clothes, and the insurance company refused to honor the claim because we lived on top of a commercial property, it was OK because God would handle it. I didn't ask God to correct anything in my life. I prayed for understanding and that his will be done.

I knew God worked in mysterious ways. I was not surprised when Ricky knocked on the door of our apartment with all of our stolen belongings in hand. I was even less surprised when my father, who'd purchased the apartment insurance for us through his agent, canceled the policy. He got the company to give us a full refund on premiums paid because they could not offer residential apartment insurance to those who lived in buildings zoned for commercial use. Nor was I surprised when our real estate agent called and told me he was able to get loan approval for a house in the largely black suburb of Harvey. Likewise, when my supervisor at the hospital told me he could not give me a promotion in title, but he did have a 7 percent raise for me, I was not surprised. God worked in mysterious ways. Life was simple when you left it to God.

I was a college graduate, the youngest member on the Deacon's Board, purchasing a home in Harvey, and was seriously considering pastoral school. I was the proud father of a bouncing baby boy who folks said was big for his age. I was happily married to a woman who believed the sun rose for us. We were happy.

Now it was hard to believe that I hadn't seen her in over four years.

"David!" Sugar's scream broke my thoughts of Regina and our past. Our path was blocked by a white limo. Behind us another white limo pulled to my bumper. I hadn't been checking my rearview mirror or my surroundings. Two armed New Day Brothers exited the front limo.

"Out!" one of them ordered.

It wasn't going to happen. There was no way I was going to surrender. They had us blocked on Seventy-fifth and Racine. To my right was a public library with a wide sidewalk in front. I cut the wheels sharply to the right, hit the gas, and went over the curb. I took the sidewalk to the corner of Seventy-sixth Street. I made a hard left down Seventy-sixth, floored the El-dog, and told Sugar to hold on. The New Day Brothers didn't expect me to run. They scattered back to their limos and gave chase. When I got to Morgan Street, I made a sharp right and headed south. I leaned on the horn. With my horn blaring, I blew three stop signs. At Eighty-fifth I swung a left. Greshim Police Station was two blocks east. I pulled directly into the lot and parked in the handicapped space next to the door. The limos paused, but continued down Eighty-fifth Street.

"Wow!" was all Sugar said. I quickly backed out the lot. I didn't want Sugar to be spotted by some eager police officer. I was alert. No one else was sneaking up on me. I took Vincennes to Eighty-seventh Street and made a right. My office sat on the corner of Eighty-seventh and Throop. I expected to see limos parked in front. There were none in sight. We parked in the back and entered through the back door.

Carol was sitting in the front. When she heard the back door open, she called my name.

"David, is that you?"

I answered her quickly. Her tone was edgy, and she was no longer one who hesitated to protect herself.

"Yeah, Carol, it's me."

Her desk was covered with newspapers, and each was opened to articles about Brother Yazz's murder. The *Chicago Defender* had the story on the front page. Carol pointed to the papers.

"They mention your name in every one of them, and his mama has been calling here every two hours looking for you. What's up, David?"

If not for the darkness of her skin, along with the small, tight braids she wore in her hair, Carol could have easily been mistaken for someone of Asian decent. Her eyes were narrow and slanted. She couldn't weigh more than 102 pounds wet. Her dress was always business attire, even though she was often the only one in the office. She was dressed in a gray, pinstriped, skirt suit with no split. Her blouse was buttoned up to the collar and it was well after five. She had a warm smile when she decided to give it, but this was not one of her smiling moments.

The newspapers obviously had her upset, and she set her narrow eyes on me waiting for an answer.

"It's a case Ricky referred to me. This is Mrs. Owens." I put my hand on the small of Sugar's back. "Brother Yazz's wife. Ricky hired me to protect her."

"Ricky hired you?" Carol stood and extended her hand to Sugar. "Pleased to meet you, Mrs. Owens. I'm sorry to hear about your husband. I've followed his work with some interest. Please have a seat." She offered a small, black director's chair that she kept in front of her desk. Carol and I both knew we needed better furniture, but neither of us wanted to do the shopping. Sugar didn't take the seat.

"Thank you, but if you could point me to your bathroom first, I'd appreciate it."

"Of course. Out this door to your left, and you will need this key." Carol handed Sugar the bathroom key. The door hadn't closed good behind Sugar before Carol got started.

"Since when did you start mixing your business with Ricky's? You know the kinds of things he is involved in, David. What were you thinking?"

"She needed my help," I heard myself mumbling.

"What?"

"She needed my help," I said with a little more authority. "We are in the protection business, and she needed protecting. Just last week you were complaining about me not bringing in any new accounts. Now we got a new account, actually two new accounts. Brother Yazz's mother hired me to find Sugar." I stood a little more erect and tried to stare her down. After all, I was the boss.

Carol sat down and I went to my desk, which was across from hers.

"Brother Yazz's mother hired you to find his wife and

Ricky hired you to protect her? Is that how it went?" Her tone was not at all close to that of a subordinate, which is what I was hoping for. The crispness of her tone told me she was gearing up for a good argument, or a debate as she liked to refer to our spats.

"Yeah, Mother Owens hired me to find Sugar. I didn't know where she was at the time."

"Who hired you first?"

"Ricky."

"Did anyone sign a contract?"

"Huh?"

"Did any of these new accounts sign a contract?"

She knew the answer, but she asked the question to imply Ricky wouldn't pay.

"No. Both were spur of the moment. But don't worry, I'll get them to sign." I spotted an envelope on my desk from my attorney. I smiled because I knew it was the partnership papers. Without Carol knowing, I had the documents drawn up to make her a full partner. It was only right. She was doing most of the work.

"Well in case you're interested, James Brown is in town for three days and we got him for all three. I assigned Keith and Kevin. He was a little upset you weren't working with him personally. I told him you were on an assignment."

She paused for a minute, for effect. She knew I handled most of the celebrity cases personally. She was flexing her muscles, assigning Keith and Kevin to a celebrity case, and now she was gearing up to argue, no, debate about her decision.

"And, we got three new nursing home pickups for shopping and check cashing. The bank approved the loan for the two new vans, but the guy at the bank wants you to play in their charity golf tournament. He signed the papers, but he made it clear that he expects you there. I got six interviews set up next week to hire two more security escorts. It would be nice if you were here.

"The following Monday we're flying to Dallas to meet with the Perkins agency for consulting. They are paying us twenty-five thousand dollars for the consultation, David. We can't afford to blow it off."

When Sugar returned from the bathroom, I took the opportunity to stand. I put the partnership papers on Carol's desk.

"If you get a minute, I need you to read these over and sign them. Sugar, follow me, please." I tried to match eyes with Carol to give her a smile about the papers, but she didn't look up. I walked Sugar back to our storage room. In the floor safe I kept five registered handguns. Sugar's record with keeping up with my pistols didn't stop me from giving her another .22 caliber. With the New Day Brothers on us the way they were, I wanted her armed. It's not my policy to arm my clients, but working against such a large number of New Day Brothers, I figured it might even the odds a little. If we got separated, at least she would be armed.

I knew I was breaking the law, but I wanted Sugar safe. The New Day Brothers who tried to stop us earlier didn't stop us to talk.

"Keep up with this one, OK?" She smiled and put the pistol in her purse with no hesitation. I walked her to the back door and told her to wait for me while I finished up with Carol. Carol was on the phone.

"Hold for one second. He's here now." She transferred the call to my desk. "It's Brother Yazz's mother."

"Hello, Mrs. Owens."

"Mr. Price, have you found her?"

"Yes, she's here with me." I signaled Carol to go get Sugar.

"Good. Things are changing, Mr. Price. I feel she may be in danger from some of the members."

"Why?"

"I don't have time to explain. I don't feel it's safe for you to bring her here. Maybe the police would be best. Can I speak with her?" I put the phone on mute and told Sugar that Mrs. Owens wanted to speak with her. She hesitated a moment, but took the receiver. I pointed to the speaker button and she pushed it.

"Mrs. Owens, here is Sugar," I said.

"Sugar?"

"Yes, Mother Owens."

"How are you, dear?"

"Making it."

"And the baby?"

"There is no baby, Mother Owens." Sugar rolled her eyes.

"Whatever you say, dear. Jamal and some of the others are acting crazy. They're saying crazy things. They say you stole from them. You need to get to the police. You have to keep the baby safe!"

"There is no baby, and I'm not going to the police. I'm going to the press. I'm going to tell the world what a lying and thieving bastard your son was. I got proof. I got copies of the ledgers!"

"Child, what are you talking about?"

"I have the books, Mother Owens. I have proof that the New Day Brotherhood is a scam. If I were you, I'd start packing and get a running start on the law."

"Child, get to the police. You don't know what you're dealing with. I didn't know. Get to safety!"

"I'm safe. You'd better get packing!" Sugar hung up the phone and looked to me. "Are you ready?"

"If you could give me and Carol a minute, I'll meet you by the back door." When Sugar was out of earshot, Carol started up.

"There is something about this, David, that's not right. Neither the mother nor the wife appears to be grieving. If I were you, I'd leave it alone, but I know you won't." I kissed Carol on the cheek.

"It will be over soon. You sign those papers?"

"I read them, but we have to talk before I sign. Being a partner is a big responsibility. Working for you is one thing. Being in business with you is totally different."

"I don't understand. I thought this would please you?"

"It does, David, but we got to get some things straight first."

"Like what?"

"The time and effort you'll be putting in. Working for you, I have no problem with doing everything. You're the boss. But if we become partners, you're going to have to become more committed, like you were when you started this business. It's a marriage, David, fifty-fifty. As your partner, I might push you harder than you want to be pushed." Now she was giving me that smile that could knock the chill out of February.

"I ain't worried about you pushing me too hard. Just sign the papers and get them to the lawyer by tomorrow, and you're welcome, partner," I said, turning away from her pleased face. With the phone still on speaker, I dialed Ricky's number and told him we were on our way to Regina's office. He said he would meet us there. I told him no, we would stop by and pick him up. Although I was upset with him, there was no reason not to have him around for Sugar's and my protection. I needed his help. Carol was shaking her head when I disconnected the call.

"That man ain't no good. I know he's been your friend forever, but Lord knows you probably his only friend. It doesn't make any sense for a married man to be so whorish. I put on my jacket whenever he comes here because

I can't stand his lecherous eyes. He looks right through a woman's clothes and his wife is good as gold. Umph! It just doesn't make any sense."

"Goodbye, Carol," I said, hurrying toward the back. I needed Ricky, and this wasn't a good time to hear about his faults. Once she got started on one, several more were sure to follow.

"Be sure he signs a contract!" she yelled at my back.

Six

Sugar agreed that going to Ricky's was a good idea, but she wanted me to promise I wouldn't bring up his deception. Driving north on Ashland Avenue, I ignored her request.

"David! I know you hear me. Please don't bring it up. You two don't need to be arguing right now. You both need to work together." I remained silent. "For me, David, please?"

I glanced in her direction and caught a quick glimpse of those big, pleading eyes.

"OK, but I'm setting him straight on something else."

"It won't be an argument, will it?"

"Naw, Sugar, it won't be an argument." Dusk settled over the city. I flipped on my parking lights and made a right on Marquette Boulevard. Damn! James Brown was in town and I was missing the assignment. One thing about James and his entourage was that they all ate well. Protecting him was easy. Everywhere he went, people loved him. Neither he nor his personal guards had any problem following my instructions. They called me not only because I was good at what I did, but also because I took them to the best soul food spots. Carol could have paged me or left me a message on the service. She was being ornery because I hadn't been in the office.

We worked well together and she was right, I did need to spend more time in the office. A year ago, I damn near lived there. Ricky pulled me out by saying I was getting old and he was gonna have to find himself a new partner, one who knew there was more to life than working. That was easy for him to say. All his businesses were doing fine and Martha made sure all his paperwork was in order.

He didn't like to admit it, but if it wasn't for her accounting knowledge and business savvy when it came to dealing with people, especially white people, he would have been bankrupt years ago.

Ricky had no patience in dealing with people, and even less patience when dealing with white people. He figured all white people were out to cheat him and he never tried to hide his feelings. He questioned loan officers like they were loan sharks. As far as he was concerned, business was war, and those with the power and the money were against those trying to get it.

His first business was a janitorial service. He figured no white companies wanted to mop up behind black business owners, and he was right. The market was wide open for him. He would have been happy with just black customers, but after Martha graduated and got pregnant again, she knew they needed to expand their customer base to continue to prosper. That meant going downtown, chasing after white dollars, and being competitive with white companies. Ricky told her no, that there were plenty of black businesses. She told him yes, plenty of small restaurants, beauty shops, and dentist offices, but with one corporate account, they could make more money with less effort and less expense.

Ricky didn't pursue the white dollars. Martha did. He didn't pursue loans from white banks. Martha did. He didn't like to admit it, but if it wasn't for Martha, he'd still be mopping rib joints, barber shops, selling dime bags of weed, and housing crap games in his mama's garage. Martha put him into the real money.

The drive to Ricky's went smoothly, with no interference from the New Day Brothers. When we parked in front of Ricky's castle, I noticed Sugar tighten her grip on the attaché case. She said the case held jewels, money, and the ledgers. Mother Owens said the Brothers accused Sugar of theft. Knowing what I knew about her, I didn't doubt it, but it wasn't my business. My business was to keep her safe and keep my own emotions in check. Martha's warning entered my mind. "You like to give, and she likes to take." Sugar held the case so tightly I heard her knuckles crack.

"Ain't nobody going to take it, Sugar, until you ready to give it up. Relax, baby."

"He might try. He might think he deserves a cut since he originally set it up. I ain't sharing this, David . . . with nobody."

"Who are you talking about, Sugar, Ricky?"

"Yes."

"I don't think so. He's only interested in the ledgers. And besides, he doesn't know about the jewels and stuff, does he?"

"I don't know what he knows."

I looked away from her and honked the horn. She was right; there was no telling what Ricky knew. Watching him descend the steps of his castle grinning, I thought about my list of suspects for Brother Yazz's murder. It was a short list, either Ricky or Sugar. I ruled out Jamal based on the grief he displayed. I ruled out Mother Owens because I felt she loved her son at one time. I included Ricky because he hated Brother Yazz and because Brother Yazz had interfered with his business. One of them did it. I was sure of that.

"Let's go in the truck!" Ricky yelled as he walked to his Expedition. I nodded to Sugar and exited my El-dog. Going in the truck made sense. It was bigger and maybe unknown to The New Day Brothers. I held the front passenger door open for Sugar, but she indicated with a nod that she wanted to sit in the back.

I wasn't at ease with the thought of her sitting behind us with a .22 caliber. She made a point of saying she wasn't sharing her loot with anybody. If there was honor amongst thieves, I hadn't seen it. The thought of Ricky and I overpowering her for her earned payoff may have entered her mind. She may have thought about putting a slug in both our heads. She smiled at my hesitancy as if she read my mind. She opened the back door for herself and climbed in.

A day earlier, if Ricky would have killed Brother Yazz, I would have been certain he would have told me. The recent information Sugar shared with me rocked that certainty. Doubt circled my thirty-year friend, and I didn't like the feeling. We'd been through too much together. All of us were seated in the truck, but Ricky hadn't started it. He turned so he could face us.

"So what's the move?" he asked.

"Straight to Regina's," I replied.

"Can I see the ledgers?" he asked Sugar.

"What ledgers?" I asked. I promised Sugar I wouldn't bring up Ricky's deception, but I didn't promise that I wouldn't get him to bring it up.

Sugar saw through my attempt and quickly interjected.

"I have them back here, Ricky. Hold on a second." I felt Sugar's gaze burn into the back of my neck. I didn't care. My best friend had played me and I wanted him to know I knew.

Sugar placed the case on the seat and flipped the locks. I turned when I heard the case open. What I saw pushed my anger for Ricky out of my mind, at least for a moment. The case was stuffed with marble-sized loose diamonds and bundles of hundred dollar bills. The ledgers were in a pocket above the loot.

Sugar said she went back to the church to get the jewels Brother Yazz gave her. I doubted Brother Yazz gave her a case full of loose diamonds. No wonder the New Day Brothers wanted her. Regina's lead about their involvement in the jewelry store robberies was more valid than she suspected. Sugar pulled the ledgers from the top pocket and snapped the case shut. She handed the ledgers to Ricky, but her eyes were on me.

She didn't look away. Her eyes said yes she stole the diamonds, yes she deserved to have them, and yes she would kill to keep them. I wondered if she had killed to get them.

"Damn, girl, was them real?" Ricky asked and damn near slobbered on himself.

"The ledgers are your business, Ricky. This case has nothing to do with you." She took her eyes from me and put them on Ricky with an expression evil enough to back Satan up a step.

"Look-a-here, baby girl, we started out in this here as partners."

"Partners? Partners? Where were you 'partner' when the bastard was raping me? Where were you 'partner' when he was beatin' my ass? Where were you? Ain't no partnership where this case is concerned. You wanted information on Brother Yazz and you got it! You ain't got shit else coming!"

I thought about the gun Sugar had and butted in.

"This is not the time to discuss partnership, friendship, or deception. We have to deal with the problems at hand, which are getting the New Day story to the press and keeping Sugar safe. Those are our priorities. Let's roll, Ricky." He wasn't happy with me butting in, but he started the Expedition and drove off.

We rode in silence for most of the ride. I should have kept it that way, but the air was too thick with anger, mine included, so I started small talk.

"The truck's got a nice ride, Ricky. Damn near as smooth as a car."

"It's awright," he answered. "I bought it to pull a boat I was gonna buy, but the deal on the cabin fell through, so I ain't buying no boat. I sorta got stuck with this truck." He didn't look at me as he spoke. His gaze focused on the traffic.

"You bought a truck to pull a boat you didn't have?" Sugar asked.

"That ain't cha business . . . stay in your place!" Ricky snapped.

"It's a free country. I can talk when I want to."

"Not to me, you cain't, not while you riding in my gotdamn truck." He fanned the ledgers next to his head. "This better be enough proof to shut them niggas down for good. If it ain't, you in my debt."

"I don't owe you shit!"

"How you figure dat? I'm paying for yo' protection."

"I can pay David myself. In case you haven't noticed, I got money."

"Oh, I noticed awright. I also noticed the nigga who all that money and jewels belongs to is dead. I noticed that real good." Ricky clicked his tongue to emphasize his point.

"What you trying to say, Ricky?"

"I ain't trying to say shit! I'm sayin' it. You killed Brother Yazz and stole his shit. Now, did 'cha understand that?"

"You know I didn't kill him."

"How I know that?" he asked and turned a corner hard, slinging Sugar across the backseat.

"'Cause you killed him or had him killed. You wanted him dead worse than me. I only wanted to get away from him. You wanted him dead!" She was sitting erect, directly behind Ricky, screaming in his ear.

"I wasn't the one seen running out the church," he said calmly.

"That's just it, Ricky," I said. "Sugar was seen by Mother Owens at the church, seen at the Greyhound station by a clerk, and seen by me at my house. You, on the other hand, were not seen or heard from since we left you at The Other Place. You didn't return any of my pages. Where were you, brother?" He looked at me briefly.

"Come on, D, I know you ain't trippin' like that? Not me and you, bro."

"Where were you, man?" I needed to know where my thirty-year friend was.

"Damn, bro, ain't this some shit? You my ace and you taking sides against me with some chick?"

"I ain't against you, man. I'm only asking where you were." He still had not looked me in the eyes. I could read Ricky's eyes. At least, I thought I could.

"Man, after y'all left me at the club, I started feelin' bad about telling Martha I was comin' straight back. She had fixed me a good dinner and Tiffany baked me a cake. I took my ass home, ate my dinner, got drunk, and went to sleep. I ain't hear your pages. Now you know Martha ain't gonna lie to you for me. If you want to, give her a call." He handed me his flip phone with a look that said he couldn't believe I doubted him. I answered with a look that said I don't care what you believe and dialed the phone. Martha said Ricky got home about ten-thirty or so and stayed in the rest of the night.

I should have been happy that his alibi checked out. I wasn't. I believed Martha, but I felt that Ricky was somehow involved. I gave him the phone back and said nothing.

"Told you it wasn't me, bro. Your new sweetheart got you barkin' up the wrong tree."

"Fuck you, Ricky!" Sugar hissed. "You did it."

Ricky pulled into the parking lot behind the *Tribune* building. Once he had his truck parked and the ignition off, he drew a .45 revolver from his belt and pointed it at Sugar. I knew by the swiftness of his movement not to say anything. He was pissed and far from rational. I wouldn't let him shoot her, but I had no choice but to let him get his point across.

"Look-a-here, lil' sis, I didn't kill the nigga, but if you keep sayin' that, I might put a slug in yo' ass, to shut you the fuck up. You gettin' awful high and mighty. Remember it was me who got your ass out the gutter! It was me who got those Jamaicans off your ass in California. It was me who sent yo' ass money to eat and live. It was my house you stayed in while you tried to get yo' life back in order. It was my contacts that got yo' funky ass business started again, and when yo' ass fell back in the gutter, it was me that sent D's brother to get yo' crackhead ass. So, lil' sis, don't forget where you come from, not for one motherfuckin' minute. You can keep them diamonds and shit, but when it's all over, don't say shit to me. Not a motherfuckin' word! Now get cha stupid ass outta my truck."

The three of us walked to the front of the *Tribune* building in silence. I expected Sugar to look hurt after Ricky cursed her out. She didn't. His words rolled off her like rain on my freshly waxed Fleetwood. Her steps were spry and she was almost grinning. I guessed she was happy that Ricky said she could keep the diamonds and cash. To me, the diamonds and cash indicated motive, and I was sure the police would see it that way. It still hadn't sunk into Sugar's head that she was the prime suspect in Brother Yazz's murder.

It was obvious that we appeared strange to the night guard on duty. Sugar was still dressed in her long, black dress. Ricky was wearing a white Adidas sweat suit with matching gym shoes. I was in a pair of yellow Pelle Pelle overalls with a white nylon undershirt. None of us were dressed for business. Luckily, Regina had cleared our admittance before we arrived. We rode the elevator up to the seventh floor. We were greeted by a chubby, blond, male receptionist who walked us down a plush corridor to Regina's office. I was impressed. The last time I met Regina at work, she sat in a cube surrounded by thirty other writers in cubes.

The office was small, but there was enough room for us all to sit in front of her desk. When we entered, she slowly placed a framed photograph face down on her desk. I figured it was one of her and the preacher. Sitting across from her, the church girl prettiness that originally attracted me to her caused me not to look directly in her eyes.

We greeted each other civilly, even shook hands before we sat. Sugar didn't hesitate once we were seated and the introductions made.

"These are the ledgers." She took them from Ricky and passed them to Regina. "There is enough proof there to back up what I'm going to tell you. I have no problem being quoted."

"What exactly will these prove?" Regina questioned. Her sandy hair was straight and to her shoulders. Her eyebrows, barely noticeable against her light complexion, were arched above her green eyes. She was dressed in a yellow, two-piece skirt suit. The yellow matched my overalls. Early in her career she seldom wore a suit, but as a staff writer I guess it was required. I still kept up with her work, read her articles, and in all fairness, I was proud. Our eyes met for a second and we both looked away.

"It proves that Brother Yazz was a crook!" Ricky loudly answered.

"Well, yes they will prove that." Sugar rolled her eyes at Ricky. "But not only Brother Yazz. The entire organization is crooked."

Regina opened the ledgers and skimmed through them. "There appears to be two sets of books here."

"Yes, exactly! You see, you can follow church-earned money and government grants for the shelter to investments in real estate and liquor stores. But there is very little money that was put back into either the shelter or the church, only enough to remain operational. And look at the salaries paid to Brother Yazz and his mother. You see it's all there. It is a scam." Sugar was exasperated and trembled as she spoke. "It's proof that he was a false prophet!" Sugar tried to calm herself. "Now, as I said, whatever you need me to do I will do. We have to put an end to it!" She was close to obtaining her goal and I understood her excitement.

"Who was the accountant?" Regina asked.

"Mother Owens and I kept the books."

"You kept the ledgers?"

"I helped."

"OK, first you need to be aware of the fact that these may incriminate you. Second, I'm not sure if it's illegal for the church to make these investments. Morally, a church should not own liquor stores, so it is a story. But whether it's legal or not, I don't know. I will have our legal and accounting department go over the ledgers. If there is something wrong, they will find it. Now while you're here, there is another issue concerning the New Day Brothers that you may be able to assist with as well. Do you know anything about the organization being involved in jewelry store robberies?" The question hung in the air like a kite, and nobody pulled it in.

I saw Sugar's grip tighten on the case.

"Robberies? The New Day Brothers? No, not to my knowledge. The only illegal activities I am aware of are in those ledgers." She appeared so sincere that I almost believed her until Ricky cleared his throat loud and long enough to draw daggers from Sugar's eyes. I remained silent. If they were going to go at it, fine with me. I figured some real information might seep out. These two had conspired against me. They had secrets, and a fight might let some of them out.

"Do you know something about the robberies, Ricky?" Regina asked.

"Naw, Gina, it was something in my throat," he answered, and turned his crooked smile on Sugar, who sat looking as innocent as a Catholic schoolgirl taking her first communion. They weren't going to let anything slip. The look on Regina's face told me she knew there was more. I was expecting her to push, but she didn't. She never let me off that easy when we were married. The slightest hint of a lie and she was all over it.

"OK, I'll have the legal and accounting departments

give these a complete review. You will hear from me tomorrow afternoon, Mrs. Owens." Regina stood and extended her hand to Sugar. "Ricky, how are Martha and the kids?" she asked once we were all standing.

"They fine, Gina. When you gonna stop by?"

"Soon." She appeared lost in thought for a minute. "You know I could use a lift to the train station if it's not too far out of your way?"

"Girl, you know betta than that. I'll take you wherever you want to go. You still in Harvey, right?" Yeah, she was still in Harvey, living in our house. I wanted to feel anger, but none came.

"Still there," she answered crisply.

"Well, that's where I'm takin' you. We can stop by and yell at Martha. She'll be happy to see you."

"I don't want to inconvenience anyone." She looked at Sugar and me.

"Girl, get your stuff and come on," Ricky answered.

"OK, I'll meet you all in the lobby."

It went better than I thought, seeing Regina again. As far as I could tell, she saw nothing between Sugar and me. Maybe in reality there was nothing to see. There was a time when I felt Regina could read my mind. If I thought about another woman, she seemed to know it. That was before Eric died. After that, I didn't care what she, God, or anyone else thought. My baby boy was dead and it was everyone's fault.

It was Regina's for not taking him to his scheduled appointment that day. It was mine for going to the gym and working out so hard that when I came home I collapsed instead of checking on him. The doctor was at fault for not telling us his heart could stop. It was God's fault for giving him a weak heart. The crib monitoring company should have had a volume loud enough to monitor breathing. Regina's mama was sleeping in the room with him, and she should have heard him stop breathing. Everyone and everything were to blame.

The majority of the blame, however, I put on Regina. The doctor might have told her something that day. He might have heard something in his heart. He might have noticed something in his breathing, something that might have saved my son's life. Regina said the appointments had become so routine that it slipped her mind. It slipped her mind, and my son was dead.

I tried not to hate her, but for months I wanted her heart to stop. I'd lie in bed and hope her chest would stop rising and falling. I couldn't touch her. I could barely talk to her. After a while, I couldn't stand to be in a room with her.

She tried to work it out. She tried to talk; I ignored her. She'd reach out to touch me; I'd move away. She'd cook my favorite meals; I'd eat at McDonald's. One of her last efforts was going to my father. That was the only time my father looked at me with disappointment. Regina arranged it so he and I would be alone in the house.

We sat in the small living room pretending to watch a Bears game. My father was always direct.

"That girl loves you, boy. Only a fool blames people for God's will."

"God didn't miss the appointment, Daddy. She did."

"And you think that appointment would have saved your son's life?"

"It couldn't have hurt."

"You think God's will is that simple, that easily understood?"

"The doctor might have found something."

"That doctor ain't God, boy. What God wanted to happen happened."

"Well I ain't got much to say to him these days either."

"Watch your mouth, boy! You ain't too old to get slapped silly. Boy, you were doing good. You were a deacon, had a new home, you were following the word of the Lord, living in his light. Did you think it was going to always be easy? What, you thought trials and tribulations were going to skip over you? Everybody goes through something, son. A man, a God-fearing man, doesn't look to blame others. Life tests us all, boy. God ain't gon put nothing on you that you can't handle. Believe me, boy, he knows what you going through."

"I don't doubt that he does, Daddy. In all his splendor, I am sure he knows exactly what I'm going through. And this may be some kind of test, but Daddy I ain't Job. I don't want God's tests or his love. I want my son. And my son might have been here with me if my wife would have taken him to the doctor. I can't see it no other way. And if God took my son, then fuck him too!"

I would rather my father slap me than give me the look he gave me. He looked like he'd lost all faith in me, like I wasn't his son, just some lunatic on the street mouthing off insanities.

"I know you don't mean it, boy, and God knows you don't mean it. I'm going to catch the rest of this game over my buddy's house. You take care how you treat that woman, boy. She loves you good."

She loved me good. I watched Regina walk from the elevator to join us in the lobby and wondered what my life would be like if I still loved her good, and if our son was alive. It was my mother, not my father who helped me not hate Regina. It was simple. She reminded me that Eric was more than my son. He was her grandson, my brothers' nephew, and Regina's son. Eric was our son, and more than just I missed him. And only a selfish man couldn't see that Regina loved him. "See her pain, David, and open your heart," is what Mama told me.

I told myself that I stopped hating her, but that didn't mean I didn't blame her. I couldn't love her anymore. We were more roommates than husband and wife. When she walked in our bedroom naked, I felt nothing. I went outside our marriage for satisfaction, and once I found it, I didn't care who knew. I slept with women who lived on the same block. I slept with sisters in the church. I slept with the prostitutes who walked the street behind our home. I used no discretion. I wanted her to find out. I wanted her to be hurt. I wanted to hurt her.

Walking through the dark parking lot to Ricky's truck, I thought about what Martha said. I had unfinished business with Regina. We needed to talk. I owed this woman an apology. It was as clear as the street light that shone ahead. I thought about grabbing her hand and slowing her down from the others. But I didn't know where to start. I couldn't simply say I was sorry. An explanation would be needed. The time wasn't right, and besides, my attention needed to be on Sugar and Ricky. Still, another thought entered my mind.

All through our marriage, I tried to change. How much had she changed for me? True, I believed change was needed in my life. I couldn't keep hanging out in the streets and be the man I believed I should be. But had she changed? Did she try to change, to better herself, or was all the changing left to me?

I caught up with Ricky and asked him for one of his cigarettes. He smiled and gave me a Newport, along with a look that said he would be stressed too if he was walking with his ex and his new girl.

Ricky and I sat in the front of the truck, Regina and Sugar in the back. I offered the front seat to both ladies, and they both refused.

"I need you to stop at the Greyhound station, Ricky. It won't take us a minute. Sugar needs to check on her alibi for the police." I turned around and caught Sugar rolling her eyes. She knew the verification of her alibi was as much for me as it was the police. Ricky agreed to stop at the bus station.

Only Sugar and I entered the bus station. She took me by the hand and guided me through the crowd to the ticket window. The young clerk, who looked like a college student working his way through school, could not have cared less about the people traveling or their destinations. He simply wanted to get them out of his line. He stood with a glued smile and cold, uncaring eyes. I didn't like him.

"Excuse me, young brother," and I had my doubts about calling him brother, "did you sell this lady a ticket last night?"

"Sir?"

"This lady here, did you sell her a ticket?" I pointed to Sugar.

"Does she have a receipt?"

"I ain't looking for a refund. I just want to know if you sold her a ticket."

"I sell hundreds of tickets a day."

Now Sugar ain't no average-looking woman. Clarence Carter would remember her.

"Boy, look at this woman and answer my question."

He looked at her twice before he answered.

"Oh, yeah, she was here last night. I sold her a ticket to Dallas, I believe."

"Thank you, boy." I called him boy because he was a long way from being a man. After I thanked him, I turned to leave, but Sugar wasn't following. She stood tapping her foot on the tile floor.

"What?" I asked.

"I want it."

"Want what?"

"My apology."

"I don't get it?" I did, but I said I didn't.

"You doubted me. I want an apology."

I pulled Sugar into my arms in front of all those people and kissed her.

"I am sorry for doubting you," I said quietly.

"OK," she whispered with eyes closed. I grabbed her hand and led her through the crowd. When we got back to the truck, which Ricky had double-parked in front of the bus station, we were both grinning.

"What's so funny?" Ricky and Regina asked.

"Nothing," we both answered.

I had kissed her for two reasons. First, to show her I no longer had doubts. The other reason was to prove to myself that the lust I felt was for her, and not Regina. Glancing back at both of them sitting side by side in the backseat of Ricky's truck, I realized what I told him yesterday was wrong. Regina was more than pretty. She was fine. She'd changed quite a bit. I must have more than glanced at her, because she gave me a smile that said thank you. Sugar must have seen it too, because she reached over the seat and put her hand on my chest.

"So where to now, David?" Her thumb flipped back and forth across my nipple. Instantly my jones responded to Sugar's touch. Regina's thank-you smile expanded into a grin. She slid on her Ray-Bans and looked out the window into the busy night traffic. It was the move of a mature, confident woman who knew she had the best hand.

"To the police, to get you straight with them," I answered. She withdrew her hand from my chest and sat back.

"The police?"

"Yeah, there is still the small matter of Brother Yazz's murder. Now that your alibi checks out, you might as well get them off your back."

"I don't want to go to the police, David."

"Why not? It's for the best."

"If she don't want to go, D, ain't no sense in making her go," Ricky said.

"What sense does that make, not going? They're looking for you. Not going ain't gonna make them go away."

"But I can go away while they figure it out. All I wanted to do was get the ledgers to the press. I've done that. I'm finished and I'm outta here. I ain't going to the police."

"What are you running from?" Regina asked.

"I ain't running from anything. I just don't want to get caught up in nothing."

"Like what?" Regina asked.

"Like nothing." She rolled her eyes at Regina. "It's just time for me to go."

"The deal was, D, you protect her until she gets the ledgers to the press. You've done that. Your job is done, man. If she wants to leave, then let her go."

"And how does that benefit you, Ricky, her leaving?"

"You don't mean that, man."

"I asked it, didn't I?"

"Look-a-here, man, I hired you for her. I can fire you for her, too!"

"Is that what you want, Sugar? You want me fired?"

"Are you going to take me to the airport, Ricky?" Sugar asked.

"I'll get you on the first thing smokin'."

"And why would you do that?" Regina asked. "The best thing is for her to go to the police. What you all are discussing is ludicrous. She'll become a fugitive for no apparent reason, unless there is something you both are hiding."

"That's it, Gina. They're hiding something! Ain't that it, Ricky?"

"Look-a-here, both of y'all can kiss my ass. Gina, you got yo' story, such as it is, and, D, all you need is yo' fee. Other than that, I don't see where none of this is y'all's business."

That made a lot of sense to me, but I needed to hear what Sugar had to say before I disassociated myself from the whole mess. "You agree with that Sugar, all I need is my fee?"

"Sounds right to me."

"Fine. Two days of one on one protection, twenty-four hundred dollars. Pay me now!" I knew Ricky had it on him. He keeps three to four grand on his person at all times. I wasn't surprised when he handed his snake skin billfold to me. I passed it to Sugar. "You better let her count it out. She's your partner." Sugar counted out twenty-four, hundred-dollar bills and gave them to me. The remainder of the drive was silent.

I wasn't thinking about anything except getting the fuck out of Ricky's truck. When he pulled alongside my El-dog, I jumped out without saying shit to any of them. Sugar followed me despite the hateful look I gave her when I saw her get out of the truck and walk behind me.

"Here's your gun." I took it without a word. "And, David, please keep this for me." She tried to give me the attaché case, but I refused. "Please, David. I'll be back to get it." Damn, she was doing more than asking me to keep her loot. She was making a reason to come back to me.

"Are you sure?" I asked her.

"Oh, yeah, and you'd better be too." She wrapped my fingers around the handle of the case. "Keep it for me, Mr. Price. Keep it safe until I come back." When she kissed me, one phrase rang in my mind. "Pussy whipped."

What I wanted to do was follow Ricky's truck, but logic and my own curiosity took over. Following the truck wouldn't give me information. I wanted to know what angle Ricky was working from. I didn't want to believe the obvious, that my thirty-year friend was the murderer and he wanted Sugar running to attract the heat. No, there had to be more to it than that. My list of suspects was too short. There had to be more. At least that's what I told myself as I directed my El-dog toward the New Day Brothers' church.

Seven

All organizations have disgruntled members, and with the New Day Brothers' leader being slain, I was sure someone was feeling lost and hopefully disillusioned. If not, I had one of the best motivations on earth, hundred-dollar bills. Ben Franklin's face had a way of opening the tightest floodgates.

Behind the New Day Brothers' church was their attached shelter. It reminded me of an airplane hanger because it was made of aluminum and tin. There was a line of about fifteen people waiting to get inside. The death of Brother Yazz didn't affect their need for shelter. The homeless in the city provided the New Day Brothers with a supply of new recruits. I turned my lights off and parked across the street. I was toying with the idea of getting in the shelter line when someone tapped on my window. I saw the red hair and red eyes of Paul Phillips, the private detective. I reached across the seat and rolled down my passenger window.

"What's up with you, Paul?"

"A little bit of this and a little bit of that. You got a minute?"

"Sure." I opened the passenger door for him.

It hadn't been a humid day, which was surprising for the end of July, but Paul smelled of perspiration. I rolled my own window all the way down.

"This is some case, aye? I never expected it to turn out like this. What started as a missing person turns into a murder, and I've got more information than I want. You know what I mean?" His gaze was fixed on the line of homeless people. "They keep coming like they don't know the man is dead. I guess his mother will keep housing them. What a strange bird she is. The whole family is strange, aye?"

I make a practice of never talking negative about my own people to white people.

"They're different. Ain't no lying about that."

"You don't know the half of it. The mother told me you found his wife."

"She turned up. I really didn't find her." Paul wanted something and he was beating around the bush.

"Yeah, I followed her from the bus station to your house this morning. Easy money, eh?"

"Easy enough."

"Mind if I smoke?"

"Knock yourself out." I thought about a cartoon in *Playboy* I saw once. Indians were farming tobacco and telling each other that now they would get them, referring to the white man and smoking. Paul said he'd followed Sugar from the bus station this morning. Maybe he was on her last night as well. I waited to hear if he saw her leaving the church.

He lit a Pall Mall with a stick match he struck off his chipped front tooth.

"You and I have worked well together in the past, aye?"

"Yeah, Paul, no problems." I wouldn't call it working together. I referred cases to him that I couldn't or wouldn't handle. He referred none to me. If I knew one black detective who wasn't a cop or former cop, I would refer the cases to him. A lot of the people I refer want nothing to do with the police, unless of course there is an immediate threat. Then they all want a policeman. Paul Phillips held the good end of the stick in our working relationship.

"And you know I respect you, aye?" The respect of a white man? I could not answer that question, because I had no point of reference. I didn't know what a white man's respect felt like. Most I met thought they were superior to me. No, I didn't think he respected me.

"Like I said, Paul, no problems."

"This case, David, it's no good. There's too much information on people I don't want information on." He was still beating around the bush, and his funk was becoming unbearable.

"What are you trying to say, Paul?"

"The mother hired me two years ago to find Sugar Greer. Did you know that?"

"No." *Two years ago? Damn, was everybody involved in this mess for years except me?* I wondered.

"The mother knew who she was the whole time. She let her son marry her, knowing who she was. The mother is sick, David, but she pays well."

"I don't get it." I thought about standing outside of the car and holding the conversation. His funky odor, along with the filterless cigarette, damn near had me gagging.

"Sugar Greer, or rather Sugar Nevins is the first preacher's daughter, Brother Yazz's daddy's illegitimate child. Her mama is the woman that killed Brother Yazz's daddy."

"What?" It didn't make any sense.

"Like I told you, the mother is sick. She knew they were half brother and sister before I found the girl. This case is no good. The sister I found didn't know where the girl was, but her husband, he knew. He helped me find her. You know him. You and him been friends a long time, aye? Richard Brown.

"He helped me find her. I found the girl, the mother paid me, and I think I'm finished. A year later the mother calls me back, tells me to follow her son's wife, which turns out to be the girl, his half sister. The mother let her son marry his own half sister…knowing who she was.

"I follow the girl and your friend is back in the picture. They're meeting two, three times a week. I give the report to the mother. She pays me and again I think I'm finished. A month ago the son calls me. He wants me to follow his wife and find out about the man she is meeting, your friend, Richard Brown."

Paul was finished beating around the bush. He didn't want Ricky on his ass. He may not have respected me or Ricky or any other black man, but he did fear one, and his name was Richard Brown.

"It was a job, David, nothing more. Your friend is a very lucky man. All his enemies disappear. I wanted to quit when I found out about the men that murdered his wife's family." He paused, I guess to gauge my reaction. I gave him none.

"I tried to quit, but the son paid me double to keep looking. I found an ex-crackhead in the Brotherhood who tells an interesting story for twenty dollars. It's a story about two young men who killed everybody but him. He said one young man found him behind the couch and spared his life. He pointed both of the men out in the pictures I took while I was following Brother Yazz's wife."

Again he stopped. I remained silent.

"Two young men righting a wrong is how I look at it. But it's more information than I need. Brother Yazz paid for the file two days ago. Now he's dead. I'm not saying what's what. What I am saying is that it was my job. I keep two files on all my cases, one for the client and one for me. I don't want a file on this case. I want to forget this case. I am not an enemy of Richard Brown. Tell him that. Here is the file." He pulled the file from under his sweaty shirt.

"All of the pictures and the name of the witness is in there. I'd appreciate a call telling me he knows I am not an enemy. If I don't get a call, I got no choice but to go to the police. I make my living in this part of the city. I can't and won't walk around scared. I don't think the mother knows about the file, but that Brother Jamal knows. He knows it all.

"It was a job, David, nothing personal. Let me know what's what before tomorrow night."

He was about to exit the car but stopped. "Well, would you look at that." He pointed to Brother Jamal peeping out of one of the church windows. "Why do you suppose he's peeping out of windows? Oh and by the way, what did you do to give Lieutenant Dixon a hard-on for you? He pulled me in this afternoon for questioning and you were the topic. He was pissed because it was a .38 revolver and not your .22-caliber that killed Brother Yazz." A .38 revolver—my mind flashed back to the .45 Ricky pulled on Sugar. Why not the .38 revolver?

"And get this, they found the holy man with his pants down around his ankles and with feces on the tip of his pecker. Draw your own conclusions, but I'll lay you odds that if they do a doo-doo test, Brother Jamal would give them a match. Don't forget, David, I ain't nobody's enemy." He slammed the door behind him, but his funk remained. I called to him.

"Hey." He bent down to the window. "You don't have to wait for a call. Ricky and I both know you aren't an enemy. You have nothing to worry about."

"Good, thank you. We work well together. See you around, aye?"

"Sure." I rolled the window up and put my eyes on the church window Jamal was peeping out of.

My mind was on Ricky. The more I found out, the worse it got for both of us. No wonder he was acting strangely. He was protecting all he had. Knowing Ricky as I did, I was certain Paul Phillips' life was in danger. It appeared Ricky was tying up loose ends to murders older than his first born, loose ends that could pull us both down.

Brother Yazz must have threatened Ricky, and Ricky was without a doubt the wrong man to threaten. Paul was justified in his fear. I was uncertain of the safety I promised him. If Ricky viewed him as a threat, it would take more than me to stop him.

I was sorting through the information Paul Phillips gave me. I saw the New Day Brothers approaching, but I was too involved in thought to consider them a threat. Sugar and Brother Yazz were half brother and sister. Brother Yazz was found with feces on his jones. Paul Phillips knew about an old shoot-out involving Ricky and myself.

I don't know why I thought of it as a shootout. It was an assassination. I doubt if either of them boys fired one shot. Ricky kicked the door in and we entered, guns blazing. I don't know who shot who. I closed my eyes and pumped my granddaddy's .32. I got the gun after granddaddy died when I was sixteen. My family went down to Atlanta to bury him. After the funeral, my father sent me in the shed to get all his father's fishing tackle. In the largest tackle box I found the .32. I kept it a secret.

Three years later, with my granddaddy's gun in hand, I was going to kill or be killed. At that age, Ricky and I were coming into our manhood. Every day the hood put us through rites of passage. When we were younger, it was gangs. They were constantly trying to recruit us, and we stood our ground with the help of my brothers.

My brothers fought to earn their respect and keep their independence in the neighborhood, and we had to fight to earn ours. They made sure we were never grossly outnumbered. Four to five boys jumping on the two of us, were not outnumbered. They intervened when it was six or more. The way they saw it, we were being taught by the best—them. Each of us had to be able to handle two dudes our age in a fistfight, and we could. After a while, we were no longer Robert and Charlie's little brothers. We were "Ricky and D," two young niggas known to thump all night.

My brothers didn't play high school sports, so neither did we. We went out for the teams, qualified, and never went back. We thought that was cool—showing them we could do it if we wanted to. We followed my brothers. They played craps, gambled two on two in hoops, pot bowled, hustled pool and chess, and played girls for whatever they could get from them. My oldest brother Charlie, the Republican, said it before DJ Quick: "If it don't make dollars, it don't make sense." He pounded that into our psyche. We made dollars and gained the reputations of hustlers. We knew hustlers, and they knew us.

Martha's mother wasn't buried a day before people in the streets started telling us who did it. The information stayed consistent. Everybody said the same two names. There was never any doubt in my mind about what we had to do, and Ricky didn't have to ask me. When he told me he was ready, nothing else was said. I got my granddaddy's gun and he got his mama's.

When Ricky kicked that door in, I closed my eyes out of fear. I was expecting to die. I was certain I was going to die. I closed my eyes so I wouldn't see it happen. When I got shot, I was going to keep my eyes closed until I saw God or one of his angels. I pumped my granddaddy's .32 until all I heard was the hammer hitting empty chambers. Ricky had to grab my hand and tell me it was over. When I opened my eyes, I saw two boys sitting on the couch. They looked like someone had splattered them with rotten tomatoes, something Ricky and I used to do a lot to other kids.

Ricky told me it was time to go, but I stood there, waiting for those boys to get up and wipe them tomatoes off their faces. It was a kitten that broke my trance. It darted across the room and behind the couch the boys were sitting on. I went to get the kitten and saw a third boy hiding behind the couch.

The kitten and the buck-eyed boy had nothing to do with the murder of Martha's parents. Only two boys broke into Martha's house, the two boys on the couch. I walked out and left the kitten, and never said a word to Ricky about the other boy.

I needed to talk to Ricky, really talk, and put all this current mess aside. I started the El-dog and was about to pull off when I noticed that the two New Day brothers were standing in front of my car with guns drawn. They escorted me into the church.

The New Day Brothers' church was not much different from hundreds of other storefront churches, simply larger. There were at least five hundred folding chairs in neat rows in front of the pulpit area. They directed me to the room to the left of the pulpit, the church office. Brother Jamal was sitting behind what I guessed was Brother Yazz's desk. I hadn't felt the air conditioner walking through the church, but the office was cold. On the wall behind him above his head was a five-foot portrait of Brother Yazz's daddy.

Whatever Brother Jamal wanted, I hoped he was brief. I had to get to Ricky quickly if I wanted to save Paul. I was expecting to be searched and disarmed. I wasn't. I waited for Brother Jamal to speak first. It was obvious he wanted to choose his words carefully. There was a chair in front of the desk, but he didn't offer me a seat. I remained standing and looked him in his face. His guards were still behind me.

"Mr. Price, do you know where Sugar is?"

"No," I said as definitive as possible, letting him know I was not afraid of him.

"I find that hard to believe, Mr. Price."

"So." I didn't fear him or the guards behind me. If push came to shove, I was certain I would be the one to walk out of the office. The guards were standing too close to defend themselves against my attack.

"You are in no position to be flip. Where is she?" The guard to my left nudged me in the back with his pistol. I ignored it. "Where is she, Mr. Price?"

"I don't know. I dropped her off a short while ago at Union Station." Brother Jamal looked to the guard to my right and he left the office.

"Have a seat." I sat and the guard to my left exited and pulled the door closed behind him. "I saw you talking with the detective. Did you find him as informative as I did?"

"He didn't tell me anything that I didn't already know."

"Really? Again I find you difficult to believe."

"Why?"

"I am aware of the information he has."

"And?"

"You knew nothing about the blood line between Sugar and Brother Yazz. Only Mother Owens and myself were privy to that."

"Not Brother Yazz?" He was in a talking mood, so I slipped in a question.

"No, of course not. He hated his father. If he knew of his mother's desire to . . . umh . . . rebirth him, shall we say, he would have been repulsed. No, that information was on a need-to-know basis, and he didn't need to know."

"Why did you?"

"Pardon?"

"Why did you need to know?"

"Oh, well I was sort of the catalyst that put Sugar and Brother Yazz together. Honestly, Mr. Price, how much do you know about Brother Yazz?"

I decided to shoot straight at him, get him riled.

"Are you asking if I knew that you and he were fuck buddies? Yeah, I knew that."

"Fuck buddies! How dare you." He was about to stand from the chair, but changed his mind and settled back. "We were lovers for years. We met in prison, and his mother had no choice but to accept it. Once I was released, I came straight to him and he accepted me with open arms. Of course we had to be discreet, but we were lovers all the same. His heart pumped to please me, and mine for him. We were much more than fuck buddies, Mr. Price."

"What about Sugar?"

"What about that bitch? She was never worthy of him." I could tell he wanted to spring out of that leather desk chair. He was the kind of man that liked to talk and walk, especially when he got excited. At least that's the type of man he appeared to be. I was certain he was a shouter in church.

"She views you as a friend."

"Of course she does. That's what she is supposed to think. I was her confidant, her shoulder to cry on in times of need. Mother Owens worked it out so we were brought into the fold at the same time.

"You see, Brother Yazz had me a little place in Hyde Park. But once Mother Owens found out, she insisted I join the Brotherhood." He fanned himself with one of those paper fans with the wooden stick handle and a picture of Elder Pastor Owens on it. There was no way he was warm. The office was freezing. He fanned himself out of habit, and he looked like a church mother doing it.

"Mother Owens approached me with such clarity of thought, I had to admire her. She approached me unbeknownst to Brother Yazz and laid out the most seductive and intricate plot I'd ever heard, and it was against her own son, my lover. God, that woman's mind excites me. I not only admired the plan that was crafted akin to one Satan himself would create, but I admired her acceptance of things to meet her goals. By things, I am specifically referring to myself." He placed his open fingers against his chest.

"She soundly believes that homosexual love is morally, spiritually, and physically wrong. But because her son and I were in love, she included me in her tangled web. That alone was enough to hook me, but the ten thousand dollars she gave me put the cap on my involvement."

"She paid you ten thousand dollars to remain her son's lover?"

"No. Pay attention, please. She paid me to be the catalyst between Sugar and my man. In retrospect, the ten thousand wasn't worth it. After the child was born, if it was male, Sugar was to be paid off and Brother Yazz and I would go back to normal. But getting him interested in Sugar was a difficult notion. You know he was gay before prison. He had no interest in fish. But a deal was a deal, and a good plot has to be executed. Do you want to hear how I got him interested in Sugar?"

"No." I swear to God I didn't. "Why does Mother Owens want such a child?"

"Open your eyes." He pointed to the large portrait above him. "She is still in love with the dead preacher; not in love, obsessed. I can understand why. If the daddy was half as good as the son, she got some lovin' good enough to keep you waiting a lifetime." Brother Jamal paused for a second, obviously thinking about his last statement. "I shouldn't be so crude. It's much deeper than that. She believes Elder Pastor Owens would have been another Dr. King if he weren't slain. She believes that in her heart.

"She expected to see the same in her son, but Brother Yazz could only talk the talk. He couldn't walk the walk. He walked on my side of the street." His smile was sweet with slyness. "A mother is always the first to know. She might try to deny it, but she knows. The more she pushed him toward what she wanted him to be, the more he secretly rebelled. That bank wasn't his first robbery, and I wasn't his first gay lover, despite what she wants to believe.

"He wanted power, but he didn't want to get it through the pulpit. But that's where he was the best. Mr. Price, if ever a man was born to be a preacher, it was him. He could turn the coldest heart warm, have an atheist looking to the sky for the Lord. Oh, sweet Jesus, the man could preach!" He closed his eyes for a second in remembrance.

"But he didn't want it. He preached for his mama. You know how the New Day Brotherhood got started? We were on the yard in Statesville and I noticed how everybody was spilt up—Muslims in one group, gangsters in another, and Christians in theirs. I told him a true leader could bring them all together. He said, 'a smooth nigga could do it, and would get rich behind it.' I thought it was something he was just saying until he started sending me copies of the news articles reporting on the New Day Brotherhood. He got out two years before me. What started as an observation, he materialized into an organization. The man was great by anyone's standards."

"Not his mother's."

"No, not his mother's." Tears formed in Jamal's eyes. He didn't bother to wipe them when they ran down his cheeks. "Only one man was great as far as she was concerned. You know she didn't have a funeral for Elder Pastor Owens, only a memorial service. His body was never seen by anyone but her. The rumor is that his body is inside that statue in her living room." He pulled his handkerchief from his gown pocket and dried his tears.

"Mr. Price, Sugar took things from here that did not belong to her, property that belongs to the board of the New Day Brothers. We want it back, and Mother Owens also wants what was taken from her—the child. If we do not retrieve what is important to us, I will solve a very old murder case for the police. I know what was in the files taken by Brother Yazz's murderer. I may not have it on paper, but I am sure what I tell the police will be enough to get them to open an investigation, especially with the name of a witness. We want back what is ours. I suggest you get busy." He tried to look stern, but he couldn't pull it off. His face was too tender.

"Did Sugar take the files?"

"No, it was not Sugar's voice. I'm not even sure it was a woman's voice. After the shots were fired, I was in no state to recall much of anything."

If he was in the room when Brother Yazz died, why didn't he see the killer?

"You didn't see the assailant?" The words left my mouth, then I remembered what Paul told me. I wasn't trying to embarrass the man.

"No. I was not in a position to see anyone. The murderer called us filthy sodomites and shot Brother Yazz in the back of the head. He fell across me on this desk." He opened his arms as if to grace the desk. "We were interrupted twice—first by his mother, then the murderer.

"After you shot your guns off in the store, Brother Yazz said it was time to end it. He came back here and called Mr. Brown. He left a message telling Mr. Brown to meet him at the church."

"What did Brother Yazz want?"

"The liquor stores and any information Mr. Brown had gathered against the New Day Brothers. Brother Yazz was willing to trade that for the files about the killings you *both* were involved in." I ignored his emphasis. He didn't scare me and he knew it.

"A blackmailing preacher?"

"No, a man of vision." The chair could no longer hold Jamal. He stood straight up after I called his lover a blackmailer. "Our time has ended, Mr. Price. Again, I suggest you get busy. The memorial services will begin tomorrow at three PM. I would like this matter settled no later than five PM tomorrow. If not, I will go to the police."

"You and every other motherfucker in this city."

"Sorry?"

"Nothing."

When I got outside I went to the pay phone on the corner and paged Ricky 911. This time he called me back.

"What's up, D?"

"Where are you?"

"In Harvey, 'bout to drop yo' ex off."

"Is Sugar still with you?"

"Yep."

"I just met with Brother Jamal and Paul Phillips. I know what's going on, man. I know about them trying to blackmail you."

"Ain't nobody tried to blackmail me, brotha."

"Stop the shit, man! I know what's going on!"

"Then you better tell me, nigga."

"Come to my house and bring Sugar. I might not be there when you get there but wait for me."

"I cain't guarantee Sugar will be with me. That's up to her."

"Bring her, Ricky, shit!" I slammed the phone down into the cradle. I knew he would bring her. I had one stop to make before I went home. I started the El-dog and pulled off. I hated it when someone tried to make me do something. I hated it even more when they were successful at it, and Brother Jamal was headed for success. Sugar was going to give him the jewels back, whether she liked it or not. If it weren't for the confusing feelings I had for her, I would have given them to him myself, right then. But I didn't want Sugar to feel like I was taking her loot from her. I was going to give her a chance to object and argue, but in the end, the jewels were going to Brother Jamal. I knew where Ricky was, so Paul Phillips was safe for the moment.

I hadn't thought about those boys for years. They killed Martha's parents, we killed them, and that was that. I didn't allow them to occupy space in my mind in the past, and I wasn't planing on allowing space in the future. It was over. They did wrong and we corrected it.

I pulled into a gas station and debated over the purchase of a pack of Newports. I hadn't bought a pack of cigarettes in over five years. I bummed one from Ricky every now and then and that was how I liked it. But now

I wanted a couple of them. I watched a crowd of young boys entering the station. Every one of them was someone's son, despite how they looked and acted. Somebody somewhere loved their droopy pants wearing asses.

Those boys from the past were someone's sons too. I'd never thought about it like that before. Those boys from the past had just become a pivotal point in my life. The thought that they were someone's children had never entered my mind until that moment. A father somewhere was missing his son because of what we did.

We didn't go to their funerals, we didn't acknowledge the fact that they had funerals. But they did. They must have. They too had parents, parents who missed them, parents who loved them, parents who felt they were taken away too soon. They were more than the murderers of Martha's parents. They were someone's sons.

My own son's funeral is a permanent fixture in my conscious thoughts. At least once a day, something reminds me of it. The color of a woman's blouse may match the baby blue lining of his coffin. A flicker of light seen out of the corner of my eye may remind me of the burning candles that were above, beneath, and around his casket. The link in a person's gold necklace may bring back the image of the gold braided handles on his casket. For me, there is nothing sadder than the sight of a child in a tiny casket. I decided against the cigarettes and drove to meet another sonless parent.

There were no guards or guard dogs in front of Mother Owens's home. I saw a dim light in the front window. When I reached to ring the bell, the door opened. Mother Owens was dressed in a long, soft, pink robe. She allowed me to enter without saying a word. I followed her into the living room.

The only light in the room was the one that lit the statue. She sat on one end of the sofa and I sat on the other. We both looked at the life-size monument to Elder Pastor Owens.

"He was a great man, Mr. Price." I didn't think she required a response, so I said nothing. "But like many great men, they produce lesser children. I once read an African proverb that said a great flame produces only ashes. Oh, how true that is.

"My son's memorial service is less than eighteen hours away and I have yet to prepare my own words. I loved him, I loved him dearly, but he was only ash from a great flame. So many problems in our community, so many people looking for a leader, and there is none to be found.

"They're all paid off and laid aside. My son was supposed to be different. In the beginning I viewed his going to jail as some divine intervention. So many of our young, black men have gone to prison. I believed God was training him to shepherd all of his flock. I even accepted his mixing of religions and his sexual perversion for the same reason. God was working with him, making him a man of the times, a man for and of the people. Sweet Jesus, I was wrong. It wasn't God working on him. It was Satan.

"My husband had vices and he prayed. We prayed that God would remove them. My son, Raymond, embraced his vices. He lived for them. He said he didn't have to ask for God's forgiveness, because God created him and God knew what he was. My God didn't create him. He belonged to another god: the god of ashes.

"I tried to blame Jamal. I tried to blame prison. I tried to blame my husband. I even blamed myself. But there is no blame. He was what he was.

"God, he could have done so much more. He was needed so badly, but he couldn't see that. He couldn't see past his own wants, his own desires. We are a community under attack, Mr. Price. I believe in my heart that

AIDS is no accident. It's too convenient. Fifty-seven percent of all cases are African American, yet we only make up 13 percent of the population.

"I heard a comedian say that the prison system was justice—just us. I couldn't laugh. Some truths are not funny. Do you know how many girls I see daily who are plagued with drug addictions they pass on to our unborn? Sugar was not a rarity. I house at least fifty Sugars. That damn crack. I remember when cocaine was a rich man's high. Funny how it got to be so affordable. I read an article yesterday that said heroin was on a comeback. Tell me, where did it go, when did it leave our community?

"We need leaders, daddies, true preachers, good men to be held up and admired. I don't have to tell you who our youth admire. I'm sure you're familiar with Nino Brown, the demigod of the nineties

"We have so few men to lead. I am designed by God to follow a man, and so are my sisters. I admire strength and sternness, and so do my sisters. These should be the characteristics of our men. They should be able to provide and protect. As a woman, I am attracted to those who can provide and protect, and so are my sisters. Now my sisters and daughters are providing for and protecting each other. Our men have been castrated by poverty and drugs. God, we are so lost, and it didn't just happen.

"Man, by nature, Mr. Price, is a dominant animal. Males of most species wage war against other males. We are under attack, and it's global. Only a paid-off fool doesn't see it. And black America is full of paid-off and doped-up fools. Do you know that our youth dance to music that tells us to kill each other? Do you know that the most popular movies among black youth are movies where we kill each other? Years ago, I read an article in one of those music magazines. It said AIDS started in Africa, and judging by the rate it's spreading through Africa, I believe it.

"Who but a paid-off or doped-up fool doesn't see the attack? I don't know which one is worse—a black man with a little money and pseudo power, who feels he is above the problems of blacks all around the world, or the brother who sticks his head in the sand by using drugs. We need leaders, Mr. Price, good, strong soldiers, men like my husband.

"He wasn't perfect, but he knew we were at war. He saw the genocide. He preached against it. He tried to inform those paid-off fools. He told them that their corporate, city, and post office jobs didn't separate them from the blacks mopping floors and digging ditches. Their homes in the suburbs didn't separate them from those dying in Africa from starvation and disease. We are one, we are all black.

"But you know blacks with a little something. Mr. Charlie let them have his old house, so they weren't that black anymore. They were sending their kids to college, so they weren't that black anymore. *Julia* was on TV, so things weren't that bad anymore. Yes, a vengeful widow's bullet killed my husband, but they, those paid-off fools, were killing him a bit at a time.

"They began to ridicule him behind his back. They called him 'Pastor X, the radical Christian.' Fools didn't know Christ was a radical. They said he was a man who didn't know when he had it good. Paid-off fools are what they were. When he died, I didn't disgrace him with one of their mock funerals.

"We held the mortgage on that church. It was our parents' homes that were mortgaged to get it. It was our dream to build a church for the people. Most of them came after it was built, paid-off fools who wanted to belong to a big church. Since they were already paid off, I laid them aside and sold the church right from under them."

I thought Mother Owens was sobbing, but she was giggling, damn near laughing.

"Mr. Price, you've got to stay a step ahead of them paid-off fools. You know this will be the second church I helped build and walked away from. The third church will be the one. It has to be. I doubt if I've got four in me. The grandson will do the work of the grandfather. Good crops come every other season. It's in the seed, my granddaddy used to say. It's all in the seed."

I hadn't noticed when I walked in, but in the dining room ten or twelve suitcases were stacked beside a casket. No way Brother Yazz was in there I told myself. The shocked expression must have shown on my face, because Mother Owens answered my unspoken question.

"No, the police will not release my son's body. We will simply hold memorial services. I am leaving the burial to Jamal and the rest of those paid-off fools. I am walking away. Well actually, we're flying."

"We?"

"Yes. I've spoken to Sugar again this evening. It appears she's come to her senses. I knew she would. The child is a survivor, as I expected her to be."

"Where to?" I wasn't surprised. Sugar wanted out of town, and Mother Owens had the resources to get her out without police interference.

"Sugar lacks concern for her own people, Mr. Price. She needs exposure to the world. She needs to learn that she is one part of a whole. I am going to start with Africa, then the Caribbean. I am not sure where we will settle in America, but believe me, it will be a highly black-populated area."

"The New Day Brotherhood?"

"For all practical purposes, it's gone. Money is being transferred as we speak. By the time we reach Ghana, we will be two very wealthy widows. Let Jamal and his band of thieves fight over the crumbs."

"Does Sugar know how wealthy?"

"Lord, yes. The girl knew the numbers darn near to the penny."

"Brother Jamal?"

"A paid-off fool, Mr. Price, and a criminal to boot. He and the board have been robbing jewelry stores. I suspect my son's demise can be attributed to his involvement. You cannot embrace evil without paying for it. I told him that. But never fear. I have set wheels into motion that will make Brother Jamal's life miserable." I was certain she was Regina's anonymous caller.

"You think Brother Jamal killed your son?"

"He or one of the other board members. The majority of them are criminals, friends of theirs from prison. After Jamal arrived, they all followed like flies to shit. It was Jamal's frantic desire to locate Sugar that caused me to pry. My son, the media hound, kept clippings of the reported robberies, along with the New Day Brotherhood articles.

"Jamal is not the brightest bulb in the pack, or the steadiest bridge in a storm. He cracked after one or two targeted questions. I drafted a letter with my attorney, which he will hand deliver to the police after Sugar and I are airborne. Oh, and Sugar suggested that a copy be delivered to your wife at the *Tribune*."

"Ex-wife."

"Sorry, Sugar didn't mention she was an ex."

"When are you meeting with Sugar?"

"We are to meet here after the service. My attorney is driving us to Gary, Indiana. He has a small charter that will fly us to New York, then we're off. He has also been instructed to take care of your fees."

"What will you do if the child Sugar carries is a girl?"

"She'll be the most dynamic female preacher in the country."

I decided not to beat around the bush. I wanted to understand why she would put half brother and sister together.

"There are a lot of things that could go wrong with mixing in the same gene pool." She didn't blink an eye or show any signs of surprise at my knowledge.

"It's God's will. Everything will be fine"

"No, I don't believe that. It wasn't God who manipulated the situation between half brother and sister."

"OK, my will."

"Does Sugar know?"

"No. Is there an additional cost for her not to know?"

"I'm not a blackmailer. I'm a security escort."

"God bless you."

"Do you trust in God?"

"Yes."

"You don't think God can make his own leaders?"

"Where are they, Mr. Price? Were they born to crack mothers? Are the seeds in some male's rectum? Are they locked up in some federal prison? Were they born with AIDS? Where are they? Desperate times call for desperate action. I know the type of man my husband was. We need his type now. I am not insane. I am lucid. I am aware of how this must sound to you, but open your eyes, your ears, and your mind. We are under attack, and we need leaders who know it. My husband knew it. His seed can help us."

She said she was lucid. I didn't see it in her gray eyes. I saw obsession. She spoke to me, but she was looking beyond me, my guess was to the future and to the past. I thought about one of my father's sayings: "If you got one foot in the past and another in the future, you're pissing all over today." Mother Owens said it would be all right if the child was born female, but I doubted that. She wanted her husband reborn.

"Raymond was born from your husband's seed," I said.

"Yes, but again, great flames produce only ash. Good crops come every other season. Two halves together will make one whole. The child will be my husband reborn. His ideas and desires will surface."

The beeper I own seldom goes off, and I often forget it's even attached to my keychain. When it went off at that moment, it startled me. I stood from the sofa, and escaped Mother Owens's obsessed gaze.

"May I use your phone?" I checked the number. It was Ricky's cell phone. He was paging me 911. Mother Owens offered me the portable phone on the coffee table. Ricky answered on the first ring.

"They got the drop on me, man!" he screamed into the phone.

"Who, what are you talking about?"

"Those New Day clowns. They took Sugar and Gina from me."

"What?"

"It just happened, man, in front of your house. I think we should go to the police, man. These dudes ain't playing with full decks. I recognized one and I know he's a nut. These some hardcore thugs, D, and it's too many of them."

If Ricky knew about the information Paul Phillips had gathered, he was certainly playing it cool.

"We can't go to the police, not yet anyway."

"Did you hear what I said? These ain't no lightweight

thugs. These motherfuckers are hardcore, career criminals, baby!"

"We can't go to the police. I'll explain when I get there. Stay put." *Click. Damn, what was Regina still doing with them?* "Excuse me, Mother Owens, I have to go."

"It's the board of directors, isn't it?"

"Yes."

"And they have Sugar?"

"Yes, and my wife."

"What can I do to help?"

"Stay by your phone."

"Maybe I should go with you. They do respect me."

"It's not about you, Mother Owens. It's about the jewels."

I had gotten in my El-dog, started it up, and was driving without cutting on my headlights when a yellow cab signaled me by blinking his lights. I honked a thank-you and cut on my lights. I didn't agree with Mother Owens's explanation of Brother Yazz's death. I couldn't see a New Day Brother killing Brother Yazz. They loved the man, and it appeared he was sharing the ill-gained wealth. I thought about what Paul Phillips said. All of Ricky's enemies disappeared. That wasn't entirely true. Sure, a couple had met with questionable ends, but they lived and operated in a questionable arena.

Ricky was not a cold-blooded killer. He reacted to threats. If he was pushed, he pushed back. He didn't kill to organize a crime family. He was not a gangster. As he liked to refer to himself, he was a businessman, doing hood business.

The reason he continued to operate illegal businesses was simple. He did it to reach young brothers. He said he did it for the money, but I knew better. The majority of Ricky's legal employees were once his illegal employees. If a young brother was good at selling weed or running a crap game, Ricky gave him the opportunity to run a liquor or grocery store. If a young brother displayed supervisory skills, Ricky gave him a cleaning crew. None of his employees stayed illegal for more than two years. If they didn't want a legitimate job, Ricky would cut them loose. As he often said, he wasn't a Don, just a black man trying to make it.

According to Ricky, young brothers want to make big money. Like every other American, the way to reach them is to give them a chance to do exactly that. Most of them would not consider a job in a small store. They would look at that as petty. But give them the opportunity to sell weed or run a crap game, then they were hustlers. And being a hustler wasn't petty.

Even though the monetary reward might be less than that of a store job, it was better to be a hustler. Ricky let them be hustlers for about a year. He let the game sink into their minds good. They experienced firsthand what the life of a hustler was like. They usually got arrested or robbed. If they got arrested, they borrowed money from Ricky for a lawyer. If they got robbed, they went to Ricky and asked for more weed on credit. Either way, they were in the hole with Ricky. The profit they made was owed to Ricky. They still had to pay their rent; they still had to eat. They still had to buy clothes, and the car still needed gas.

This was when Ricky suggested that maybe the hustle wasn't for him. Ricky offered the young brother a legitimate job. If he took it, all past debts were removed, giving him an opportunity to really start over. If he said no, Ricky cut him off—no weed, no crap games. When the boys failed as hustlers, Ricky said they were open to suggestions, unless they really wanted to be criminals. Those who wanted to be criminals, he left to the streets.

From what I had observed, the harder ones were those

who were successful in the game, the ones who don't get arrested or robbed. These boys gave Ricky a run for his money. They saw no reason to stop hustling, because, in their eyes, the game was paying off. They were paying their rent. They were driving nice cars and wearing nice clothes. His approach with them was different, and if it weren't for Martha, he wouldn't be able to do it. He showed them the white world, real money.

He brought them to his home, showed them the fruits of his honest labor. He opened his wallet and flashed his platinum American Express. He drove them downtown in his twelve-cylinder Jaguar to meet with his corporate clients and his real-estate attorneys. He flew them to New York for lunch and took them to the bank were they could see his true net worth.

He told them:

> ". . . a hustle is just that, a hustle. One always has to sweat when they hustle. Real money is not made from hustling. You have to slow down and plan. A hustle gives you no time for planning. You're always on the move, hustling, sweating, and pushing yourself for pennies, dodging the police, the stickup man, other jealous hustlers, and for what? Rent money, car note money? Real money is made when you have a plan and you have to slow down to plan. It's hard to plan with sweat in your eyes and the police on your ass. What happens when a hustler gets old and he cain't run like he used to? He spent his youth running, not planning. He dies broke and alone. He dies living in transient hotels and standing on the corners begging for wine money.
>
> If you want to keep hustling, fine, but you won't do it with me. With me, you're going to have to start making real money, you're going to have to start

using your brain instead of your back and your legs. I'll get richer with you planning than with you hustling, and so will you."

He offered these boys a manager's position and 10 percent of the store's profit. They were largely responsible for him owning 80 percent of the neighborhood liquor and grocery stores on the south side of the city. With the young men's desire for more, and Martha's expertise in business, Ricky's success was certain to continue. That was, if his involvement with the young men of the past didn't stop his involvement with the young men of the present.

Eight

I pulled behind Ricky's truck, which was parked in front of my house. He and my brother were sitting on the front steps. They both had keys, but both were afraid of my dogs. My brother looked pretty good. He looked clean and was wearing some new jeans and a red Bulls jersey. I thought about what Sugar said. Ricky promised my brother and her enough money to get high for the rest of their lives.

When I got on the porch, I looked into my brother's face. He wasn't high and his skin was clear. My brother only looked this good when he was sober and on the wagon for a day or two. I couldn't stop my smile and I had to hug him.

"You looking good, Robert," I said after the embrace.

"Thanks, man. You can thank that sweet, little thing you had staying with you the other day."

I opened the front door and led them to the kitchen. Yin and Yang brought up the rear.

"You gonna put these mutts outside?" Ricky asked.

"They live here," I answered. I was still irritated with

Ricky. We all sat down at the table. "How is Sugar responsible for you looking good?" I asked my brother.

"She asked me if I was tired of being sick and tired, if I was tired of looking like warmed over shit, if I was tired of begging people for money and not being a man. Then she gave me fifty dollars and slammed the door in my face.

"Now you got to understand, David, me and her been knowing each other a little while. I knew her when she was nasty, and like Biggie Smalls said, she went from 'nasty to classy.' I wasn't expecting to see her when I knocked on your door. I sho wasn't expecting to see her in one of grandmama's dresses. She put me in the mind of grandma and mama. And when she slammed the door—man, it fucked with me.

"I am tired of not being a man. I came by here tonight to tell y'all that I'm going into the Salvation Army's six-month treatment program. Shit, man, I'm damn near fifty-years-old. More than half my life is gone. I'ma spend the rest of it sober. I know I told you and the rest of the family I'ma get high till I die, but I don't want to die high. I want to die like a man. I was kinda hoping after the six months was over you would let me stay here with you and Sugar. But Ricky told me about all the shit that was going on. So now, little brother, I'm here to help you. After we get all this shit straight, you and I can talk, OK?"

I had waited all my adult life to hear my brother say words similar to those. He was not one of those addicts who was always quitting. Like he said, he told people he was going to get high until he died. He never said he needed help to quit. He said he simply wasn't quitting. As far as he was concerned, the only problem he had with drugs was getting them when he wanted them. I wanted to be happy for him, but my mind wouldn't allow it. The current situation was paramount.

"Thank you, Robert. I do need your help. This situation's got me going, bro. I don't know where to turn. What I thought was, wasn't. It's all fucked up now." I put my attention on Ricky. "Ricky, what was Regina still doing with y'all?"

"She wanted to come, D." He offered no further explanation despite the probing look I gave him. I wanted to ask him how the hell he let them get the drop on him, how the hell he let them take two women out of his truck.

"So what do they want?" I asked his big-headed ass instead.

"The jewels."

"When and where?"

"Tonight at the church."

"Fine. We take them their loot and it's over." I was telling him how I wanted it to go.

"You think so?" He said it like he knew something I didn't.

"Yeah. All they want is the loot, right?" If he knew something, I wanted to hear it.

"What about what Sugar wants?"

"Who gives a fuck what Sugar wants!" I did, but I wasn't telling him that. "Ricky, I'm sure Sugar would rather be alive than have that loot. And besides, she will be well taken care of."

"What do you mean?"

"She cut a deal with Mother Owens. They're leaving for Africa tomorrow." I saw the surprise in his eyes. Sugar had not included him in on that. He looked away from me. "You got what you wanted. Brother Yazz is dead."

"I didn't kill him, D."

I didn't ask him if he killed Brother Yazz. I don't ask questions I already know the answers to. His constant denial made him guiltier in my eyes.

"I know why you did it, Ricky."

"I didn't do it, man."

"Ricky, I know about the file. Paul Phillips gave me his copy." I threw it on the table. "I understand, man. I might have done the same. You were saving your family."

"What the fuck are you talkin' about?" He opened the file and started flipping through it.

"Nothing. Just a murder, no murders, and deception. You, Robert, and Sugar played me. Y'all set it up and I followed."

"Hold up, bro." My brother looked up from the table. "I didn't set you up in shit. I found Sugar for Ricky and that was it. All this other shit, I ain't got shit to do with." He looked to Ricky. "Tell him, man." The file had Ricky's complete attention. "Tell him, man!"

"Robert wasn't involved in the play on Brother Yazz." Ricky looked up from the file to me. "And, man, all I did to you was get you to take the files to Regina. The play was on Brother Yazz. Ain't nobody did shit to you, except not include you. I don't know what the fuck you gettin' all huffy about. You startin' to sound like some lil' ole bitch!" He wasn't smilin' when he said that. He said it with disgust. "Have you seen what's in this shit, and you still stuck on bullshit!?"

"You didn't know about that file, Ricky?"

"This is new to me, nigga!"

"New to you? You know what that's about."

"Yeah, I know now! Shit, but until you laid it on the table I thought this here was between me and you." He looked at me as if I had let something slip out, like I was traitor or some loose-lipped child. His look was actually threatening. I looked away from him. His lies and mind games were turning my stomach.

Sitting in my grandmama's kitchen I realized how important this room was to me. It was a simple kitchen not unlike hundreds of others. The table where the three of us sat was where I proposed to Regina. It was where I ate the birthday treats my grandmama cooked for me. It was where Regina sat and pumped milk from her breast for Eric's bottles. He was a greedy boy and I couldn't wait to see him sit at this table and eat the special birthday meals I knew my grandmama would prepare for him.

It was only a room, only a table, but for some reason I didn't want to sit at it and hear my thirty-year friend lie to me. Lies weren't told at this table. People who sat at this table shared unconditional love, family love. I never lied sitting at it, and, as far as I know, I was never lied to sitting at it. Ricky was going through the file like he didn't know it existed. Direct was how I talked to people I cared about.

"You can stop with the charade, man. That's the information Paul Phillips gathered about the shooting of those boys that killed Martha's parents. You know, the boys we slaughtered." My brothers, along with most of the hustlers in the hood suspected we did it, but neither them nor anyone else had ever asked us about it. "You remember those boys, don't you, Ricky?"

"You know damn well I remember them. What the fuck is wrong with you, man?" The look on his face said something was wrong with me, like I was the one full of shit.

"Nothing that a little soul cleansing wouldn't help. Maybe thirty years in prison might do it. What do you think, Ricky? You think we'll get off easy with thirty years?" My brother was silent. He fixed his gaze on the center of the table. I knew he didn't want me to ask him what he thought. He wanted to be a silent observer, so I left him alone. "You think Martha and them young thugs could run your businesses for thirty years? In thirty years, all your kids will be good and grown. Businesses running without you, kids grown, best buddy in prison with you—you wouldn't want that. You would kill to stop that from happening, wouldn't you, Ricky?"

"It wasn't no damn witness! All this is bullshit, D, some kind of scam." Ricky was yelling and jerking his head. A clump of his finger-waved hair had broken free of the pomade and was standing erect in the center of his head.

With each jerk of Ricky's big-ass head, the hairs wavered. Ricky was talkin' in his harshest tone, his eyes were threatening, and his yellow jaws were turning red, but that damn clump of hair was wavering and having a good ass time. I turned to my brother to see if he saw it. He did, and he was biting his lip to keep from laughing. I didn't think it was funny enough to laugh at, but my brother has laughed out loud at funerals, so I knew it wouldn't be long before he broke out in a full laugh at Ricky's expense, especially if Ricky continued to look as angry as he did.

"Robert, I need you to do me a favor, bro." There was no way he was going to the church with us. It would be just his luck to decide to live drug free and then get killed. "I need you to take the dogs out for a little air, man." I was expecting him to object, but he was up and out in a second. He damn near forgot the dogs.

"There was a witness," I told Ricky after my brother and the dogs went out the back. "A little buck-eyed, snot-nosed kid. He was hiding behind the couch. I saw him and he saw us. It's time to pay the piper, Ricky. I paid, but I guess it wasn't enough."

"D, baby, you losin' it. We don't owe nothing behind that shit! Them boys was rabid dogs and we shot 'em down." He looked into my eyes for me to agree with him, but I couldn't. "That's it, and that's all. Rabid dogs!"

"They was boys, Ricky, somebody's sons. It's an eye for an eye, and I blamed Regina. Sweet Jesus, I blamed her. It was me, man. My sin. An eye for an eye, a son for a son. We got to pay the piper."

"Nigga, you done lost your motherfuckin' mind." The look on Ricky's face told me he truly thought I had.

"No, I haven't."

"Who did you say gave you this shit? Paul Phillips? That sleazy ass, white boy is trying to scam us. I hope you didn't admit to shit, the bastard. He won't make it through the week, threatenin' me and mine!" Ricky slammed his fist to the table.

"I told him he had nothing to worry about from us, and I meant that." I put my eyes sternly in Ricky's. "Besides, the threat ain't coming from him. He gave us what he had. The file you killed Brother Yazz for is the problem. Brother Jamal saw it before you took it."

"Man, look-a-here, I'ma tell you this one last time, I didn't kill the bastard!"

"Where's your .38 revolver?"

"Right here!" Ricky pulled the gun from his pants and slammed it on the table.

"Has it been fired?"

"Hell no." I picked the gun up and smelled the barrel.

"It smells like it's been fired."

"You crazy as hell." Ricky snatched the gun and sniffed it. He was playing it to the hilt. "Man, I ain't fired this gun. Why it smells like it, I don't know."

"How come you didn't have it with you earlier?"

"When?"

"In the truck, on the way to Regina's job. You pulled a .45 on Sugar."

"Damn, D, I reached for it in the closet, but I couldn't find it. I was in a hurry and I overlooked it. I grabbed the .45 from the lamp table. When I went back home for Regina to see Martha and the kids, the gun was in my jacket. No big deal."

"Why is it smelling?"

"Man, I didn't kill the bastard. Maybe you smelling the new gun oil I'm using."

I didn't justify that with a real response.

"Whatever, man. It don't make that big a difference anyway. We going to jail for killing them boys. Too many people know about it."

"Who is too many?"

"Shit, ain't no telling who Paul Phillips told. He's scared shitless. You can also include Brother Jamal and probably the whole New Day Brotherhood board. And let's not forget the snot-nosed kid turned crackhead. Paul said he tells the story for twenty dollars. We can expect to be blackmailed by somebody for the rest of our days. I don't know about you, but I ain't up to paying some scum for the rest of my life."

"The hell you don't know about me! A motherfucker ain't blackmailing me the first time. I say we go in there and tie up all these gotdamn loose ends, including your buddy Paul Phillips."

"I'm through killing, Ricky."

"Then stay your ass home. Give me the loot and I'll deal with it!"

The ride to the New Day Brotherhood's church was brief and silent. My plan was simple—give them the jewels, take my women, and leave. I smiled at my own thought—my women. Neither were mine. One had been, and the other I was beginning to feel was unobtainable, too crafty even for me. Life was a game for Sugar, like chess. Everyone around her were pieces, and she was playing against either God or herself, both being equal. No, I couldn't claim either as my woman.

What had me a bit perplexed was Sugar leaving her loot with me while planning to hook up with Mother Owens and her widow's wealth. Was her plan to leave Mother Owens and return to me after she'd secured her fortune, or was she planning on seeing me before she left? Why have Ricky drop her off at the airport? Was she playing him as well? Were they even going to the airport? How much did Ricky really know? The latter question had me more than perplexed. I was good and pissed due to the fact that my ability to trust and read my thirty-year friend had faded with his involvement in this case.

Ricky drove his truck down Sixty-third Street with a determined look on his face. The streetlights flipped through the dark truck. He believed it was all about to end—no more threats, no more loose ends. I didn't think so. I expected sins of the past to wreck our present and future life. Freeing Sugar and Regina was all I expected from the meeting. Matter of fact, that was all I was going to allow. No one else was going to die.

Brother Yazz, such as he was, did not deserve to die because of our past actions. Who did Ricky think he was? Neither he nor I was above God's law. We killed, and one way or another, we had to pay for it. "Things done in the dark find the light," was another one of my daddy's sayings.

I couldn't continue to justify the death of those boys based on their actions against Martha's parents. They were not rabid dogs. They were boys. If they were rabid dogs, what were we? I looked across to my thirty-year friend and saw the determination in his face, and I felt his need for closure, his need to protect his family and his life at all costs. If we were taking this drive before Eric's death, I would have agreed with him, but now, I knew the pain of losing a son.

"Ricky," I slowed my voice and tried to remove any anger from my tone, "we are in and out of there—no mess, no fuss. I'll give them the loot and we leave with the women, understand?" I could see him contemplating his answer.

"D, why you punkin' out on me, man?"

"What!"

"Why are you punkin' out? You know what this situation calls for. Look-a-here, I don't want blood on my hands, but I ain't gonna punk out. I got a life, D, a wife and family. I ain't got to explain how important both are to me. You trippin' about dem boys."

"We killed two boys, Ricky. How am I tripping?'

"You lettin' time cloud your memory and you puttin' two thangs together that don't go together. Eric's death had nothin' to do with dem boys! Dem boys was scum. You forgot how they killed Martha's parents, how they butchered them. You forgot about her daddy lying up in da hospital with his balls cut off and his manhood sliced down the middle. You forgot about the screwdriver they poked his eye out with. You forgot how they broke each one of his fingers tryin' to get him to tell them the combination to the safe. You forgot they tied him to a chair and made him watch while they raped his wife, Martha's mama!

"You forgot they clipped off her nipples with a toenail clipper after they got the safe open! You forgot that man lay up in that hospital for three days with that shit eatin' on his mind until it finally killed him. Them niggas was scum! Don't forget that, D. We did the world a favor.

"Look-a-here, man, I'm sorry about callin' you a punk, but you ain't been thinkin' clearly. Maybe I should'na put Sugar on you. You ain't been yourself since you met her. You ain't never turned against me, bro. What's up?"

I heard him, but I didn't answer. He was partially right. I had forgotten about the brutal way Martha's parents were killed. His words brought back the original anger and disgust I felt when it first happened.

Ricky and I were both crazed with anger then. We couldn't accept that people we knew could be killed in such a way, not in our neighborhood, not in our hood. When Martha's father died, we had to do something. Ricky didn't have to convince me. I wanted to kill them. At that time, those boys were scum and we were the eradicators.

Martha's mother was one of the mothers of our hood. I didn't know her personally, but it didn't matter. She was above all the bullshit of the streets. The streets had no business touching her. Those boys had no right touching her or anybody else's mama. Mothers have always been sacred. I know brothers who will shoot you for cursing around their mothers. Mothers were not to be raped or beaten. No woman or girl should be raped. And no man should have to watch while the mother of his children is raped.

Ricky told me Martha's daddy cried when he told him what happened. He was powerless to save his own wife. He gave them the money after they broke his fingers. They didn't have to mess with his wife. But they did, and we had killed them because of it.

"Do you remember how you felt back then, man?" I asked Ricky the question without looking at him.

"When, D?"

"Before we killed them . . . and after we killed them."

Ricky pulled out his box of Newports and offered me one. I declined. He lit himself one and inhaled deeply.

"Before, I was pissed and hurt. I was thinking it could'a

been my mama or your mama. It could'a been anybody's mama. I didn't want it to happen again. When I left Martha's daddy's hospital room, I knew what I was gonna do, and he did too. I saw it in the eye he had left.

"He never thought too much of me. When he found out me and Martha was going out, he told her the apple didn't fall too far from the tree. He was talkin' about my old man. But that day in that room, he didn't care what tree I fell from. He looked at me man to man and heart to heart. We knew each other's minds. He died knowing them niggas was good as dead. Afterward, I felt like a man, like I had passed the test of life. I was proud. I felt invincible, strong, and mean as hell. I killed. I could bring death to those that fucked with me. I discovered power. My whole world changed when we walked out of that house. I knew nobody would ever punk me and live.

"It felt good, D. It really did. I made somethin' right in the world. I corrected somethin'. I balanced the scales. I had power. But you know what, I wasn't a man yet. I had to learn how not to use the power. It's a lot of shit that goes along with this dick, and you cain't rush life's teachin'.

"I thought I was a man after we killed them niggas. I thought I was a man after I got my first piece of ass. I thought I was a man after I got married. I thought I was a man after Dave was born. I thought I was a man when I started providin' real good for my family. But it ain't one thing. It's a whole bunch of things that goes into the makin' of a man. What about you, D? How did you feel before and after?"

I wasn't ready to answer.

"You know we ain't never talked about it before, not like this, asking each other how it felt. Why is that, man?" I asked.

"I don't know, D. Ain't never had a reason."

"Why now?"

" 'Cause we fixin' to kill some mo' niggas."

"No we ain't."

"We'll see." I wanted one of his Newports, but I didn't ask.

"Before we killed them, I wanted them dead, and I wanted to be a part of it. Like you, I felt it could have been my mama or yours. The savageness is what enraged me. I was still raging when you kicked in that door. I was raging as I stood there pumping my granddaddy's pistol."

"Yeah, with your eyes closed." He chuckled.

"Man, I knew I wasn't going to get out of that room alive, but my anger wouldn't let me not do anything. I had to react to the shit they did. Scared or not, I had to do something. They raped a mother and made a father watch. They deserved to die, and I wanted to be a part of their deaths. Anger and fear together—people say you can't feel both at the same time. They just don't know. That's a deadly combination. That's how I felt before it happened—mad and scared.

"Afterward, I was confused. Once the deed was done, the rage left me. Remember when we were kids and we used to bomb people with rotten tomatoes? That's how those boys looked to me. Like some kids we had just bombed. But they didn't wipe that shit off, did they, Ricky?" I wasn't looking at him. I was looking out the window at the passing street lampposts. "You might not remember, but a cat ran across the room and went behind the couch. I went to get it, and saw another kid. I left him because the rage was gone. We got who we came for.

"Later I didn't feel tough, mean, powerful, or manly. I felt weak, drained, and deceived. I remember thinking about what my grandmama told me about the devil. After he uses you, she said, he throws you aside like a dirty sock. The sock feels good while the foot is inside, nice and full. But when the foot is finished with the sock, it leaves and the sock is hollow, empty, and flat. It's left with the funk of the foot's presence. That's how I felt, like an empty, flat, funky sock, kicked aside. I felt that the devil filled me with anger, and now that the deed was done, he left me, and his funk was all over me."

"Damn! That's fucked up, D. No wonder you didn't want to go to the whorehouse with me. You didn't have no foot in your sock." Ricky was trying to make a joke, but I ignored it.

"Do you believe in God, Ricky?"

"I leave all that God shit to Martha."

"Do you believe in the devil?"

"All that's part of that God shit, Martha's department. I believe in what I can see, touch, and feel. If I can make it happen, it's real. If I cain't, fuck it. People spend their lives waiting for God. I spend mine livin'. Prime example, these New Day fools. Brother Yazz been milkin' 'em all along. If they didn't have their eyes to the sky lookin' for somethin', they would'a saw his ass comin'. I did. From day one, I knew the bastard wasn't right. But my young nigga, Thomas, he didn't see him coming. He went hook, line, and sinker for the whole scam, him and a couple of my other young brothers.

"They had the nerve to tell me he was like me. He helped young brothers get their lives together. They had me wrong, so I knew they had him wrong. I help young brothers make me more money. That's it and that's all. Ain't shit charitable about what I do. It's business, business in the hood.

"I had those boys' heads on right. They wasn't lookin'

for nobody to do shit for them. They was doing it themselves. They wasn't lookin' to the sky for Jesus to help. They had they eyes at eye level, watching the white man and jealous niggas, too. They had their minds on business until Brother Yazz started fuckin' with them. They should'a saw him comin', but he made them look up so he could stick his slimy ass hands in their pockets.

"Talkin' all that brotherly love and heaven shit. Fuck an afterlife. Niggas got to do fo' now. That's what I teach young brothers, to get they money now. But that smooth ass snake got inside their heads with that heaven shit.

"You know Thomas was my protégé, the first young nigga from the streets I took under my wing. It hurt my heart to hear him talkin' that silly ass afterlife shit. He was managing two stores and had about ten hot dog cart boys workin' under him. That's why Brother Yazz went after him. The boy had focus and the ability to lead.

"Thomas turned all his money over to that nigga, told me it was only worldly possessions, and he was now concerned with his soul. I told him if Brother Yazz was interested in saving his soul, then leave his money to me to manage. Told me no, said I was too worldly.

"When my protege woke up, he was broke. He came to me and told me I was right and that Brother Yazz was full of shit. I told him he could have his stores back, but he said no, he had something else going on. The next day he was killed in one of those jewelry store holdups.

"D, I ain't gonna lie to you, I hated Brother Yazz and my plan was to kill him. But I was gonna get his liquor stores first. His dying fucked up my plan. I didn't kill him, D. I wanted to, but it was gonna be in my time. I wanted to break his ass first.

"I wanted people to see that he and his God wasn't shit. Do I believe in God? Man, I would be fucked up if I did. Look how fucked up believing in God has you and all them New Day fools."

"How do you lump me in with the New Day Brothers? I didn't follow Brother Yazz."

"No, but you lookin' to the sky. You want somethin' to come save you, somethin' to make your life better, some understanding of life. It ain't to be understood. It's to be lived. Niggas go crazy lookin' for understandin'. How the fuck you gonna understand what you don't control? For years, you been tryin' to understand why your son died.

"An eye for an eye, a son for a son—man, that's the dumbest shit you ever said. If believing in God got you thinking your son's death was some kind of repayment for killing that scum, then, D, you fucked in the head. Your son was born with a weak heart and he died. Them niggas killed and raped Martha's mama and they died. If you would'na shot them niggas, your son would'a still been born with a weak heart. That's life. You cain't figure it out. All you can do is live it. And, man, that stuff your grandmama told you about the devil, you let that stop you from feelin' good about killin' that scum! Man, wasn't no gotdamn devil in that room, just sick ass niggas that needed killin'. We was the men that did it."

"I ain't sick, Ricky. You just don't understand. Your son is still alive."

"Look-a-here, let me tell you somethin', somethin' you obviously ain't never thought about and somethin' I swore I would never tell you. I thought you felt the same way I did about killin' them niggas, but I think this here gonna help your lookin' to the sky ass out.

"When we walked in that room, nigga, yo' eyes was closed. And motherfucker, back in dem days, you couldn't hit the side of a barn with your eyes open. Think about what I'm tellin' you, and remember what you saw when you opened your eyes. Remember them holes in the wall above the couch?

"Remember why you couldn't hit the side of a barn? You always let the gun kick up. You shot high in them days, nigga. Your weak ass couldn't hold a gun steady if your life depended on it. So tell me, nigga, how did you manage to shoot two niggas sitting low on a couch with your eyes closed? Huh? That kinda fucks up your eye for an eye, son for a son theory, don't it? Nigga, the only thing you killed in that room was wall plaster."

"What?"

"Nigga, you ain't killed nobody. You shot the wall! I didn't have the heart to tell you."

"I d-i-d-n'-t . . . I didn't?"

"No, you didn't. Damn, I should'a told your ass a long time ago, but I thought I was doing you a favor lettin' you think you did it."

"A favor?"

"Look-a-here, we at the church. You goin' in or what?" I hadn't noticed the truck was stopped and parked. Ricky flicked his cigarette butt out the window and lit another. He had his big-ass head turned to the church, the back of his finger-waved head facing me. I balled my right hand into a fist and knocked the hell out of him. He yelled, but before he could turn around, my 9 mm was drawn and placed against his temple.

"You yellow ass bastard." He hated being called yellow. "What kind of motherfucking favor did you think you was doing for me? The only thing that is saving your life right now is my belief in God, you fucking heathen! When this here shit is over, nigga, I don't know you." I holstered my pistol, grabbed Sugar's case, and left his gotdamn truck without another word.

I felt Ricky behind me, but I didn't turn around to acknowledge him. I yanked the church doors open and walked in without pausing. The church was bright, damn bright. Every light in the place was on. Seven New Day Brothers sat in the pulpit area. They were no longer dressed in white gowns. They were dressed like the street thugs that they really were, wearing baseball caps, nylon short sets, tailor-made, two-piece vest suits with no shirts, jeans, silk T-shirts, and plenty of gold chains. Standing in front of the altar was Brother Jamal and Mother Owens. Brother Jamal was the only one who still wore his New Day attire.

I wasn't surprised at Mother Owens's attendance. She wanted Sugar safe. Sugar and Regina were sitting in front of Jamal and Mother Owens, facing Ricky and myself. I approached with no fear. I was going to get this over with as quickly as possible. Brother Jamal met me in the center aisle, two steps away from Sugar and Regina.

"Here you go." I handed him the case and stepped around him to the women. Ricky stayed in the aisle. I helped both women up and began walking toward the front door.

"One second." Brother Jamal stopped us. He put the case in one of the folding chairs and opened it up. He smiled at the contents. "You're free to go."

The words weren't out his mouth good when I heard the pump of a shotgun followed by a 12-gauge explosion that splattered Brother Jamal's face in the front rows of chairs. I didn't run. I stood there firmly holding both Sugar's and Regina's hands. We weren't going to get picked off running. Mother Owens joined us as we turned around to face the board of the New Day Brothers.

The one who killed Brother Jamal was standing, grinning from ear to ear. He hopped over the altar, and closed and grabbed the case.

"Stupid motherfucker never even saw it coming. Ain't

no faggots ridin' with this crew." He returned to the seven. "Brothers, the time to jet out is now. Damn, almost forgot, Lil Willie, ain't you got some business with these here gentlemen?"

A guy no bigger than Carol, wearing black jeans and a blue, silk T-shirt stood from the choir bench.

"Not both of 'em. Just the big, yellow one. Come up here, ya yellow bastard," he said to Ricky. Ricky approached and stood beside me. "Don't remember me, do ya?"

I did. I knew his bucked eyes.

"You killed my brother Josh and his nigga Betoo. Shot 'em down like dogs." He drew his pistol and took aim. Mother Owens stepped in front of Ricky. "Bitch, I'll drop you first. Don't make me no difference."

I released Sugar's and Regina's hands. Mother Owens spoke.

"You have your stolen goods. Leave us alone."

"Ain't that easy," the one with the shotgun said. "Like your son said, we all come to our end. You folks have come to yours. Sugar, get on up here, girl. Ain't no sense in your fine ass dying with them. I always wanted me some of that."

"Fuck you!" It wasn't the smartest reply, but I loved that in her.

The chairs offered us no cover. We were sitting ducks with one exception. Ricky and I were armed. Only two of them had their guns drawn. It would be close, but there was a chance. I glanced over to Ricky. His eyes darted to the prayer room to the left, some seven feet away. I put my eyes on the shotgun-carrying thug. Ricky put his on Lil Willie. It was confirmed. I had the shotgun, Ricky had Lil Willie, and then we would break for the prayer room. Nothing like having a friend when you were cornered.

I was about to draw my 9 mm's.

"Ain't this a motherfuckin' bitch!" someone said from

the back of the church. "Me and my dogs come in here to pray for Brother Yazz's soul and see folks holding guns in the church. What kind of mess is this?"

My brother Robert played the part of a drunk staggering through chairs making his way toward us. Yin and Yang were behind him. I signaled them into attack mode. Now all they required was a target.

"Bobby, you in here?" I be damned if Carol didn't come in behind him. "Bobby, come the heck outta here. These church people ain't got no time for your drunk butt. Wow! Y'all got guns. Bobby, come on here!" She advanced while she was calling Robert. The shotgun pumped. I threw Sugar and Regina to the floor. I gave Yin and Yang center targets with the command to kill, and damn if it wasn't on. And this time my eyes were open.

The 9 mm I had pulled on Ricky in the truck was stuck. Only one gun came from the holster. I had to bend down to my ankle for the .22 caliber. I nailed the thug with the shotgun with my second shot. I caught the baseball cap going for his pistol, and Ricky and I caught a silk shirt taking aim. Mother Owens fell from taking one in the chest. The guy in the black jeans and blue, silk t-shirt got her, and Carol nailed him clean in the forehead. Yin and Yang each had one by the throat. Lil Willie had a bead on me. I thought he had me, but Ricky nailed his ass. Damn, it was over. I had a 9 mm in one hand and a .22 caliber in the other. I dropped them both.

I bent down to Mother Owens, but she was gone. One bullet had torn her chest open, and another opened her forehead. I rolled her over so Sugar wouldn't see. Regina was on the floor trembling and praying with her hands covering her eyes. I crawled to her and pulled her into my arms.

"Baby, it's over. Come on, baby, get up. It's over." She

didn't respond. She kept her hands pressed to her ears. I cradled her in my arms like a child. "Come on, baby, we got to go."

I saw Sugar's jeweled hands pick up my guns, then I heard her tell everybody to stay where they were. When I looked up she was standing over me with the case in hand.

"Leave her and come with me. Come on, David, leave that bitch there! We got over three million dollars in diamonds. It's ours. Don't nobody know about this shit. Come with me, David. Now!"

I tried to ignore her and continued to comfort Regina.

"You don't care about that bitch! How could you? You love me. You know it! Stop playing games and come on."

"I ain't leaving, Sugar. Ain't nobody going to stop you. Take them jewels and go ahead."

"You would stay with her, instead of leaving with me? We will be rich, David. I ain't gonna let you do this to yourself. Get up!"

"No." There was no way I was leaving Regina like she was.

"If you don't get up and leave with me, I'll shoot her ass dead, David, I swear. You love me." I didn't love her. She was beautiful, but I didn't love her.

"I'm staying. Y'all leave Sugar alone. Go on now and catch that plane to Gary. Nobody can stop you," I yelled. "Let her leave with them jewels. Ricky, give her your truck, you hear me!"

"Yeah, D, I hear you."

"She can't have you. You're mine. I told you that. Come on, let's go. I'm not playing. She had you and couldn't keep you. You mine now! Get your ass up and come on."

"I'm staying, Sugar." When I looked up at her again

she was crying. Crying, for me? I didn't believe it. I guess she misread the doubt in my face for rejection, because her face turned stone cold.

"She's not going to want you without a dick! I told you, the dick was mine!" I saw her take aim, and the lights went out.

Nine

I think I hate hospitals, but it's kind of hard to hate something or someone you need. I want to see Ricky. I don't want to ask the nurses or the doctors anything without talking to one of my people first. I surely don't want to talk to the police before I speak to one of them. The cavalry came through. Like Daddy said, "A black man needs his friends." Man, my mouth is dry. I feel like a gotdamn mummy.

"David, are you awake?" A familiar voice, but I can't turn my head.

"Carol?" My voice is hoarse as hell.

"Don't talk, David. She shot you in the neck. The doctor was worried that your voice box would be strained. Of course he didn't call it a voice box."

I got to ask her about my jones. I'm trying to call her over, but my arms ain't working for shit.

"Don't try to move, David. I know you want to know what happened. Everybody is fine, well except that crazy bitch. Ricky shot her ass. Your brother and Ricky are waiting for the hospital to call and notify them that you're here. I acted like I found out by accident that you were here. Your brother and Ricky told me not to come, but you know ain't no man telling me nothing these days.

"Your brother tried to tell me not to come over to your house after he told me you and Ricky went to the church. He was going to sit there and wait for you to come back. But I ain't letting no man tell me nothing. Suppose we would have waited? You would have been dead. After I got to your house, I made him go to the church with me. We brought the dogs because neither one of us knew the command to send them back in the house, and they got in the car with us. Them dogs know more than you give them credit for, David.

"The doctor said you ain't paralyzed. None of the bullets hit your spine. But they got you strapped down to prevent movement. There is still one bullet in you in your thigh. They're calling your family to get permission to operate.

"Why did she want to shoot you in your thing, David? Never mind, don't answer that. In case you don't know, she missed."

"Thank you, Jesus!"

"David, don't talk. Let me see what else would you want to know."

"Sugar's dead?"

"Yeah, she's dead. We had to leave you there. We were too scared to move you. Ricky and your brother fixed the church up as best they could. They tried to make it look like they killed each other. Looks like it's working so far. The news reported a shootout where all the assailants but one died. Don't say anything to anyone until you talk to Ricky or Robert."

Man, I didn't want Sugar to die. She should'a left. I'm tired. I hear Ricky and Robert talkin', but my eyes won't open.

* * *

I recognize the voices—cops. It's Detectives Dixon and Lee, and they're talking as if I'm in a coma or something. I can't tell who is who, and I'm not going to open my eyes.

"We don't really need shit from him. He was only there protecting the preacher's wife."

"Fucked that up, didn't he?"

"Doctor said it might be weeks or days."

"Shit, we can match the shooters with the weapons."

"We need lab help for that."

"Well I know we shouldn't have a problem with that. You still boning old girl in the lab, ain't you?"

"Yeah. You sure we got all the guns?"

"Yeah. If we don't, we will. The only problem is a dog killed two of them."

"That ain't no problem. Find a dog and shoot out his teeth."

"We still need a statement from him. We don't know who shot him."

"I got the statement from him when I came in. He said the gangbanger with the gold tooth shot him. Didn't you hear him?"

"Yeah, I heard it. How you know he's gonna go along with it?"

"Because we the police and this spade knows it. He got street nigga all over him. He knows what time it is."

"What about that little Chinese-looking woman that came and got his car?

"She works for this spade. He tells her to be cool, she's cool. Trust me, ain't gonna be no flack behind this one. Shit, we probably covering up some of his shit anyway. Hey, don't this spade own some killer dogs?"

"Yeah, that's right."

"I'm telling you he ain't gon' say shit. And when he wakes up, we gonna let him know he owes us. Old ass street nigga like him should be good for a lead or two."

"You can keep dealing with street people if you want to, but after this case I'm getting my bars. We got the jewelry store robbers and the jewels. We got the murderer of a prominent religious figure and ain't got to spend a dime for a trial. The big shots are happy, and we are the cops bringing the good news."

"I didn't think that Brother Jamal had murder in him."

"The .38 revolver was found in his hand. It had to be his. I told you a long time ago, find the lover and you found the killer."

"Please, you thought this man here did it."

"That's when I thought him and the preacher's wife was fucking. Same principle. Find the lover."

"The doctor said he woke up what, a day ago?"

"Yeah, something like that."

"Fuck him. We going with what we got. It can't get no better."

The room is dark and the oxygen mask is off my face. I can move my right arm. I feel the bandage around my neck. I'm reaching for my jones. It's there.

Somebody is washing my face. It's a pretty little cherry nurse, one of those dark-skinned sisters with a deep, red tone. I see the straw she's putting in my mouth. Best damn apple juice I ever tasted.

"See, he has your eyes."

Regina and Eric are standing over me. The doctor must have OK'd pain killers because I'm tripping.

"Wake your lazy ass up!" It's Ricky. I feel like I'm smiling. I want to raise my hand and give him the finger.

"David?" It's Martha. I'm propped up in a sitting position. I feel pretty good. The pretty little cherry nurse is taking out the wash basin and smiling at me. She washed me up all over. I got to smile back at her. What else can I do? I got two big bandages on my chest, one on my neck, one over each pec, and one on my right thigh. It could have been much worse. Martha's smiling at me, taking inventory. She looks like shit. Her eyes are puffy and red, and her hair is halfway combed.

"You been in and out for three days. The doctor told us you would come around today. How you feeling?"

"Fine." I sound old and rusty, but it doesn't hurt to talk. "Open the drapes and let me see the sun."

"It's dark outside, David. I got the night shift. Ricky just left. He said you woke up earlier and tried to flip him off. He's been sitting with you, David. He's worried silly. He said you think he killed Brother Yazz."

"It ain't important. It's over. How you feeling about Sugar?"

"She's in a better place. How you feeling about her?"

"I will miss her, ain't no lying about that."

"Me too. You want to hear something funny? Well maybe not funny, but to show you how life is? I met with the lawyers from Brother Yazz's estate."

"And?"

"Neither he nor his mother had family alive. The bulk of the estate may be left to Sugar. And get this, she named me beneficiary in her will. If they don't find any other relatives, we might inherit quite a bit."

"Liquor stores too?"

"That's the same thing Ricky asked. He was so tickled when the lawyer said yes."

"Damn, I bet he was."

"David?"

"Yeah, Martha."

"Ricky didn't kill that filthy sodomite." Tears are rolling from her eyes. "Although I can understand why you think he would. He would kill to protect what we've worked so hard for, what the Lord has blessed us with, but he didn't do it, David.

"He and I have really been talking since you been in here." She's pulling tissue from her purse. "All these years he thought I didn't know about those animals that killed my folks. Everybody knew y'all did it, and I loved you both for it—my heroes. Do you have you any idea how much I have depended on you two over the years? When Ricky couldn't provide, you did. I know who bought those school clothes for the kids when we couldn't rub two nickels together. I need and love both of y'all.

"If a woman is lucky, David, she finds one man that will kill and die for her. For a woman to have two is truly a blessing. And, David, I am a woman who protects her blessings.

"Brother Yazz called my house and told me to tell my husband that if he didn't meet with him that night, both you and Ricky were going to jail. I went over there to talk to him.

"The church doors were open and I walked in. Oh sweet Jesus, help me through it. I saw a light coming from a room, so I walked into it. I didn't go there to shoot him, David, but I brought the gun because Ricky says it's better to be safe than sorry. When I walked in and saw what he was doing to that young man . . . and in a church, I couldn't help it. I pointed and squeezed like Ricky taught me.

"I went to help the young man who I thought was being molested, but stopped in my tracks when I heard him calling Brother Yazz terms of endearment. It made me change what I been calling Ricky all these years.

When I got to the desk I saw the open folder with pictures of you, Ricky, and Sugar. I grabbed it and fled.

"I started to throw the gun away, but I didn't know what to tell Ricky if he asked about it. You know how he is about that gun. I kept it for a day, then I put it back in his jacket.

"I prayed and talked to my God about it. My God is good and he is a forgiving and loving God. Don't forget that, David. In my heart I trust that God has forgiven me. I didn't mean to kill Brother Yazz, and God knows it.

"Well, that's all I got to say, David. I love you. Goodnight, baby. I'ma go on downstairs and check for Regina. She's been picking me up after she gets off work. I sit in the car while she runs up and checks on you. We developed a little routine since you been hospitalized. You bringing us all closer. It's good having her around. You need to talk to her. You have more unfinished business with her than I imagined. God has blessed you, David." She's giving me a sad smile. I lean up for her kiss.

I watch the door close behind her. I owe Ricky an apology, but I know we will never speak of Brother Yazz's murder. My mouth tastes like my breath is stinking and Regina might be on her way up. I feel the stubble covering my face and head. The IV is hooked up to a stationary machine. Walking to the bathroom mirror is out. On the stand next to the bed I see a Bible that looks a lot like the one I left at Regina's house the day I left her, the one my parents gave us.

The door opens again slowly.

It's a little boy. He's walking up to me.

"Hi. Mommy said you sick."

Damn, I know who he is.

"A little bit."

He's climbing up in the bed. He is sitting on the thigh with the big Band-Aid, but I don't move him.

"Mommy said you're my daddy."

"That's right." His eyes are clear and beautiful, so much like Eric's were.

"Where you been?" he asks.

"Looking for you."

About the Author

Tony Lindsay was born and raised in Chicago which explains his love for the city that is captured in every novel. He currently lives with his wife and three daughters in northwest Indiana very close to the Chicagoland area. He was educated at the University of Illinois majoring in Psychology. Directly after college he worked extensively in the mental health profession counseling adolescents. Later he switched careers and went into advertising sales where he worked for local Chicago newspapers: *N'DIGO* and *Sun Times*. Today, Tony is working on writing his next novel while managing his property management company LFL Realty.

PREVIEW

One Dead Lawyer

A David Price Mystery

By

Tony Lindsay

Coming December 2007

I am not a man who often resorts to violence. The fact is, being Black, six feet two and two hundred fifty pounds plus with a shaved head, I try to avoid the violent reaction because so many people expect it from Black males. There are, however, situations when a brother does what a brother got to do. Attorney Randolph Peal and I found ourselves in such a situation.

I was holding him with my left arm wrapped around his neck. My right hand held my .9mm pistol to his temple. I wanted to kill him because, in my soul, I was certain that he either had them killed or did it himself.

We were on the Persian rug that covered the floor area in front of his large, leather-padded desk. I tighten my arm around his neck. From kneeling behind him, I could see the bald spot on the top of his narrow head. Dandruff had formed around the roots of his remaining dishwater blond hair. I moved the pistol from his temple to the bald spot.

I wanted to blow a hole in his head, to scatter his

brains across the fancy rug and buffed wood floor. I wanted to see his blood splatter as theirs had. I wanted to end his shyster's life . . . but I didn't. Not because my desire for his death lessened, but because I was hit hard on my own head from behind.

I came to and the sun is shining bright into my eyes. I flip down the passenger visor. I am in the front seat of my best friend Ricky's Ford Expedition. He's sitting in the driver's seat, and behind me is my ex-wife Regina. There is an orange-sized lump growing on the back of my head, and Ricky's .38 pistol is out from under his black linen short-sleeve shirt and on the seat next to him. The short suit he's wearing is actually nice; why he chose to wear it with a pair of dressy baby-blue alligator shoes is beyond me.

Ricky Brown is well over three hundred and fifty pounds and at least six feet three inches tall; he doesn't do much to exert himself, so seeing him labor for breath has me wondering. My guess is his labored breathing is from carrying me out of the lawyer's office, and I'm also thinking I can credit him with the growing lump on my head. His eyes are focused on the police squad cars in front of the lawyer's building. There are at least six.

We are parked downtown Chicago across the street from the monstrously large city hall building on the corner of LaSalle and Randolph. The lawyer's office is in the high-rise on the far south corner. This side of the street in lined with high-rise buildings. Regina reaches over my shoulder from the back seat and drops my .9mm in my lap. She doesn't say a word to me. Downtown shoppers and workers walk up and down LaSalle Street staring and looking back at the squad cars. My own alertness is kicking in, and the squads have my attention as well.

"Are they here for me?" I ask.

"What da fuck do you think? Of course they here fo' yo' ass. Ya cain't go up in no big time lawyers office and put a pistol to his head. What da fuck was ya thinkin'? We agreed to a plan. Man, ya got to stop thinkin' wid ya heart. Shit. We'll be lucky to get da hell away from down here." His words are directed to me, but his gaze remains on the squad cars and police officers piling out of them.

My buddy Ricky has a big head—a huge head. Last week we went to Bacon's hat shop on 47th Street and he was measured at an eight and a half. Me and the hat maker shared a good laugh at his expense, and to make matters worse, Ricky draws attention to his three-quarters-of-a-watermelon-sized head by continuing to wear his hair in a slicked down process with finger waves.

"Look-a-here, D. I'm too old fo' stupid shit. And goin' up in there was some stupid shit! We had his ass lock, stock, and barrel. All ya had to do was follow da plan. Goin' up in there was just plain stupid!"

I have no reply. He's right. It was stupid, but there are times when stupidity is satisfying, and having that shyster at the end of my .9mm was very satisfying. It was very satisfying indeed. Admittedly, seeing his eyes buck, feeling him tremble in my grasp, watching his urine spread down his pants leg and hearing him whimper for his life pleased me.

"Man, what is ya grinnin' about?" Ricky sees my satisfied smile. "Dis situation ain't funny. You's sick; ya sittin' here damn near laughin', and dem damn cops up da block lookin' fo' yo' ass. I sho' wish you would tell me what's funny."

The good thing about good friends is you communicate beyond spoken words. His words were harsh, but once Ricky sees the grin on my face he too starts to grin.

Without me saying a word, he feels my satisfaction. His fat, round, yellow face gives way to full, toothy smile.

"Man I gots to know; was dat piss stainin' da leg of dat fine suit? Did ya make dat man piss his pants, D? I gots to know."

Before I can answer Ricky, Regina cuts me off by announcing, "I'm calling him."

"What?" Ricky and I both ask, turning around in our seats to face her thin, bright, non-smiling face.

"I'm calling him. We need to let him know we have some leverage in case he is thinking of giving the police your name." Before either of us can object, she opens her tiny phone and dials his number. I rub the sore lump on the back of my head. My whole head begins to throb harder.

This summer has been a hot one; Ricky has the air conditioner on maximum, but as I rest my head against the passenger window, I can still feel the afternoon heat outside. "Regina Price for Attorney Peal . . . I'm aware he is in a meeting, Veronica, but put me through anyway . . . Randolph, this is Regina. Yes, of course I'm fine. I have nothing to fear from David or his friend, but I cannot say the same for you. What I'm saying is that if you give David's name or description to the police, they will act in accordance. Of course I'm not threatening you . . . It's not matter of whose side I am on; it's a simple matter of you not turning him over to the authorities or pressing any type of charges . . . I am really not concerned with how this looks to you . . . Yes, things have changed . . . Dinner? . . . Tonight, it's a possibility . . . call me around eight. Goodbye."

Again I turn around in my seat to face her. I must not have heard her right. "Did you agree to dinner with that murdering bastard?"

"Yes, because I don't know that he killed anyone. That

is your suspicion." She answers quickly with her emerald eyes rolling away from my accusing gaze and out the window. "And I also got him to agree to not give you over to the police, which is more to the point of our current situation."

Her two-piece business suit, a soft summer white, buttoned to the collar, goes well with the 'stay out of my business' attitude she's offering me. The throbbing lump on the back of my head is increasing in pain looking at the snide, 'ain't nobodies business if I do' expression on her face. Her eyes roll back to me.

"I would expect a little more gratitude considering I just saved you from jail."

Although the street is filled with people, although the afternoon sun is beaming through the spaces between the thick high-rise buildings, and although Ricky is in the truck with us, in my mind I am in a dark tunnel with Regina and the tiny cell phone she used to call that shyster.

I see my hand I snatch the phone from her. The truck door opens, and I began stomping the tiny phone into the concrete sidewalk. The downtown strollers scatter away from the spectacle of me demolishing every bit of her tiny phone and stomping it to smithereens.

When I get back in the truck, Ricky is bent over his steering wheel laughing at my adolescent display of anger.

Regina remains cool in the back seat.

"That phone retailed for three hundred and seventy-five dollars. I expect payment in full."

I hear her, but Sharpton will be wearing dreads and Whoopie will be in a perm before I pay her a dime for that phone. This whole situation is her fault—hers and hers alone. And to think, I really thought we had a chance of getting back together. I must have been trippin'.

"Ricky, drop me at my car, man. I'm in the indoor parking lot on Adams."

Sliding into my Cadillac DTS, I notice the date, Wed. August 13, on my cell phone screen. The phone is in a hands-free mount attached under the dash. Tomorrow is my mother's birthday. Maybe I'll fly out to Arizona next week and surprise her and Daddy; I been promising them a visit for over a year.

The DTS starts right up. This black-on-black in black sedan is by far the best Caddy I have ever owned. I traded both my Fleetwood Brougham and El-dog for it. All I want and need right now is one car. I am tired of maintaining two and three cars. Besides, even if I still had both of them, all I would drive would be this one. This Caddy rolls.

The kid loved it too. The kid. Damn, I was starting to like him again. Only a heartless, soulless person could kill a child or a person so threatened that they would forsake what's right for self-preservation. I believe this is the case with Attorney Randolph Peal, the man whose head I just had my pistol to.

He did kill them. I'd bet my right arm on it, and if Ricky hadn't stopped me, I would have ended it. No more Black people dying at his hands. With Attorney Randolph Peal it's not a Black/White thing. With him, it's a green thing; a wealth thing. He killed them to maintain his wealthy status. The sick bastard.

In the short time it takes me to exit the parking lot, it has gotten to a comfortable seventy-two degrees in the sedan, and Miles' trumpet lead in "Green Haze" is trying hard to mellow me out. I rest my head easily against the headrest, conscious of the lump. It remains sore, but the throbbing is gone. The subtlety of the headrest's soft leather provides an almost therapeutic touch.

Pulling onto Adams street I stop and say a quick thank-you prayer; thanking God for having Ricky stop me, thanking Him for not letting the police catch us coming out of the lawyer's office, and I thank Him again for my son.